W9-CEM-786

# *Point of no return*

Marie closed her eyes. "So, let me make sure I understand this," she said. "Our parents look the same, but they're actually about sixteen inside?"

"That is correct," said Ozzie. "But there may be another problem."

"What's that?"

"The poof point," replied Ozzie.

"The poof point?"

"Yes. You see, your parents may not be done regressing. They may keep going backward in age, until they hit the age of zero."

"The poof point?"

"Yes. It's the point when they go so far back that they just go 'poof.' "

*Other Bullseye Books you will enjoy:*

*Germy Blew* <u>The Bugle</u> by Rebecca C. Jones
*Germy Blew It—Again!* by Rebecca C. Jones
*Into the Dream* by William Sleator
*The Tiny Parents* by Ellen Weiss and Mel Friedman
*Weird Henry Berg* by Sarah Sargent

# the poof point

# the poof point

by
**ELLEN WEISS**
and
**MEL FRIEDMAN**

**Bullseye Books • Random House**
**New York**

A BULLSEYE BOOK PUBLISHED BY RANDOM HOUSE, INC.
Copyright © 1992 by Ellen Weiss and Mel Friedman
Cover art copyright © 1992 by Mark Buehner

All rights reserved under International and Pan-American Copyright
Conventions. Published in the United States by Random House, Inc., New York,
and simultaneously in Canada by Random House of Canada Limited, Toronto.
Originally published as a Borzoi Book by Alfred A. Knopf, Inc., in 1992.

Library of Congress Catalog Card Number: 91-34765
ISBN: 0-679-82272-0
RL: 4.8
First Bullseye Books edition: September 1993

Manufactured in the United States of America    10 9 8 7 6 5 4 3 2 1

New York, Toronto, London, Sydney, Auckland

*For Stephanie*

# CONTENTS

# 1   *POP!*

Marie Bicker was awake. Even though her eyes weren't open yet, she was definitely not sleeping anymore. Because of the sound. It was coming from far away, and though Marie tried to ignore it, the sound would not let her drift off to sleep again. No way.

What was it? Marie rubbed her sleepy eyes, sat up in bed, and listened. Ah. Now she recognized it. It was yelling. Mildred Grackle, the Bickers' next-door neighbor, was yelling her head off outside. Her voice was loud enough to be heard clear on the other side of Brooklyn.

"Open this door!" she shrieked. "Norton Bicker, I know you're in there! Marigold! Open up!"

Marie lay still, waiting to hear whether either of her parents was going to open the door.

Then she heard her brother, Eddie, open his bedroom door across the hallway. "Marie," he called. "I think you better wake up."

Marie came out of her room, still buttoning her shirt. "What time is it?" she mumbled.

"Seven thirty-two," Eddie said, checking the grandfather clock in the hallway.

"That means it's really seven thirty," said Marie. "Mom's been at it again. She's been setting the clocks two minutes ahead."

Aside from the faint sound of distant traffic, everything was quiet in the tall, narrow brownstone. Basil, the old basset hound, snored softly at the top of the stairs.

Outside, Mildred started yelling again. "Norton! Marigold! This is your next-door neighbor! Open the door immediately, or I will call the *police!* You're *inventing* something in there again—I know you are!"

"Seven thirty on a Sunday morning," Marie groaned. "It's not human. Especially during summer vacation."

There was a quiet moment as Mildred seemed to be figuring out what to shriek next, and in this pause Eddie and Marie became aware of another noise. This noise was coming from inside their own house. *Pop,* it went. *Pop, pop, pop.*

"What is *that?*" whispered Eddie.

"I don't know," said Marie. "Sounds like it's coming from the kitchen."

"Uh-oh," said Eddie. "Are you thinking what I'm thinking?"

"Something about Mom and Dad and some crazy new invention?"

"Yup."

"Where are they?" Marie asked through clenched teeth. "They're not up here, are they?"

Eddie walked over to the door of their parents' bedroom and stuck his head in. "Nope," he said.

"That means they're working on something in the basement," said Marie. "I knew it. We'd better go down and see what they've done."

They hurried down the stairs and into the kitchen, where the door to the basement was. But before they got to it, Marie motioned Eddie to stop.

"Listen," she whispered.

*Pop. Pop, pop, pop.*

"It's coming from the cabinet," said Eddie quietly. "Where the dishes are."

"Norton! Marigold! I want to talk to you!" Mildred screeched. Marie and Eddie could see her witchlike figure hopping up and down beyond the frosted glass of the back door.

Mildred Grackle looked a lot like the Wicked Witch of the West. (Except when she was wearing her pink hair rollers. Then she looked more like a Martian.) In personality, she was also a lot like the Wicked Witch of the West, and she hated the Bickers with a deep and festering hatred. She had lived next door to them for many, many years, and every year she hated them more. In fairness to Mildred, the truth was that somehow Norton and Marigold's experiments always ended up having surprising and bad effects on Mildred's life.

Marie went over to the top of the basement stairs and called down into the murky darkness. "Mom! Dad! You'd better come up here!"

"Can't stop now!" called the voice of Marigold Bicker. "Your father has screwed up the wiring again, and everything is a mess!"

"I know everything is a mess!" called Marie. "You have to come upstairs, right now! It's an emergency!"

Marigold came up the stairs, followed by Norton. Marie silently pointed to the back door, and Mildred's silhouette. Her mother took a deep breath, straightened her bathrobe with great dignity, walked to the door, and flung it open.

"Mildred," she said. "How nice to see you."

Mildred had her fist in the air, ready to pound on the door again. Her wiry hair, wrapped around curlers, seemed to emit sparks. Her eyes flashed like live coals.

"Can I help you?" asked Marigold. "Is there a problem?"

Mildred's mouth twitched. Then her enormous nose twitched. Then her furry eyebrows twitched.

Finally she was able to speak. "Problem? Problem? Only a little, teeny, tiny one," she spat, clasping her hands tightly to keep them from Marigold's throat. "You know my collection of china figurines? My . . . *priceless* . . . figurines?" Her voice broke. "Well," she continued, "ten minutes ago, I woke up and all my figurines were . . . popping. One after the other. They were just exploding, all by themselves. My milkmaids, my little puppies, my shepherds and all their sheep, my Mother Goose that came all the way from Guam—everything. Four hundred and seventeen china figurines. Thirty years' worth of collecting. Gone, in one morning. All gone. Dust." She broke down, and Marigold tried to put a comforting arm around her.

*"Don't you touch me!"* screamed Mildred. "It's your fault, I know it! It's something you're doing over here, one of your crackpot inventions!" She angrily wiped the tears from her cheek with the sleeve of her raincoat, and her curlers bobbed up and down. "Now, you listen to me," she said,

7

poking a bony finger into Marigold's chest. "You're going to pay for all my figurines. And you're going to stop ruining my life with all your inventions, too. That little shrinking episode was no picnic, let me tell you. I'm still a quarter of an inch shorter than I used to be, thanks to you. You know what you people are? You're nightmare neighbors!"

And then she left.

"Whew," said Eddie after the door had slammed shut.

The popping noise continued from the cabinets.

"What are you doing down there, anyway?" Marie asked her mother.

"We're fooling around with a new device, something really big," said Norton. "Something that's definitely going to win us a Nobel Prize. We're just having a little trouble getting it to work right."

"Dad!" cried Marie. "Mom! I can't believe you're inventing something new! Didn't we all get into enough trouble last time, with the Proton Enlarger? It made you two and a half inches tall! It almost got you *killed,* for God's sake! Plus it shrank Mildred."

"That's true," said Norton, "but there was

8

some pretty creative science going on in the Proton Enlarger, even if it didn't work right. Don't forget, we're going to be awarded the Oopsie in two weeks. That's no small thing."

"That's right," agreed Marigold. "The Oopsie Award is the most coveted prize in all of inventordom. Besides, you don't need to worry about this new invention. We've almost got it figured out." Then she shot a look at Norton. "If your father wouldn't keep doing things wrong, everything would be fine."

"Listen to her," said Norton in a voice dripping with sarcasm. "Of course, *she* never does anything wrong. *She* never miswires the proton confabulator. Oh, no. *She* never reverses the vector field."

"Oh, put a lid on it, Dr. Einstein!" Marigold retorted. "That little trick you pulled this morning with the variable electrostatic polarizer—"

"I did not!" Norton interrupted.

"Did too!"

"Did not!"

"Did too did too did too!"

"Stop fighting, would you!" cried Marie. "I can't stand it! All I know is, something you're doing is making a lot of trouble."

She walked over to a kitchen cabinet and

opened it. Inside, an unusual thing was happening. The dishes were exploding. *Pop,* went each dish in the stack. *Pop,* went the teacups, one by one. *Pop,* went the soup bowls. A flying piece of bowl almost hit Marie in the face. She shrieked and ducked.

*POP,* went a big platter. After it exploded, the smashed bits of china hung in midair for a second, and then fell.

Norton and Marigold peered into the cabinet.

"Interesting," said Norton.

"Oops," said Marigold.

For a minute, nobody talked, and Marie became aware of another sound in the house besides dishes popping. It was a high-pitched whine, so high and quiet that she hadn't even realized it was there until now.

Norton paced the length of the kitchen, thinking out loud. "Has to be the sound the new invention is emitting," he said. "Must be the exact frequency to break china, and only china."

Now Marigold was pacing right in step beside him. Up and down, up and down they walked, scratching their chins. "Maybe if we changed the wave inducer," she said.

"No, that would mess up the vector field," he replied, deep in thought.

"Hmmm," she said. "Maybe if we increased the power . . ."

"Might work," he said.

"*What?*" said Marie. "Increase the power? What if the *house* explodes?"

"What if *you* exploded instead of the china?" asked Eddie with his usual detached curiosity.

"Even if they don't explode, Mildred is going to come in here someday and murder us all in our sleep," said Marie. She wheeled on her parents. "Why don't you just forget about all your stupid inventions? All they've ever done is cause us grief."

"Don't be silly," said Marigold. "Our inventions are interesting and useful. And this one is especially interesting and useful."

"What is it?" asked Marie disgustedly. "An electronic sock-sorter?"

"No, dear," said Marigold as she headed back to the basement. "It's a time machine."

# 2 THE TIME HUM

A few minutes later, Eddie and Marie were dressed and sitting in the kitchen eating cereal for breakfast.

"A time machine," said Marie. "That's great. That's wonderful. Even better than last time. Last time they almost turned into atoms, and this time they're going to get marooned in the Stone Age, chewing on dinosaur drumsticks."

"There weren't any dinosaurs left in the Stone Age," said Eddie, balancing a fork and a spoon on his glass.

"Don't be dumb. You know what I mean," said Marie.

"Hey, look at this," said Eddie. "I can get this spoon and this fork to balance on the tip of this knife without falling down."

"Eddie, you drive me so crazy!" said Marie. "You're just as bad as they are! Doesn't it bother you that we have dinks for parents? They wear weird clothes, they invent weird things, they think weird thoughts! Aren't you even *embarrassed?* Don't you want to have a normal house you can bring your friends to?"

"You always ask me that," said Eddie, adding two Cheerios to his balancing sculpture.

Of course, Marie knew the conversation was futile. It wasn't just that she was twelve and he was nine; she and Eddie would always be different, even when she was eighty-six and he was eighty-three. All Marie wanted was to be regular—have regular friends, read books, keep her room neat, have a regular life. She even looked more regular than he did: She had long honey-blond hair, large hazel eyes, nice straight teeth, and a nose that would have been pretty good, Marie thought, if it were just a bit smaller.

Eddie couldn't care less about normalness. He had no problem with being extremely short for his age. His glasses usually had tape holding them together, and he didn't care if his curly blond hair was standing straight up in spots, or if his buttons were in all the wrong buttonholes, or if he was half an hour late to school. He didn't even mind the mortifying fact that he and his sister were named after famous scientists (Edison Newton Bicker for him, Marie Curie Bicker for her). All he cared about was the stuff he was interested in: how things worked, why they worked, what happened if you took them apart. His parents' strange and usually disastrous experiments in the basement didn't worry him much—they just interested him. If Norton and Marigold got stranded in the Stone Age, Eddie would be very interested in that, too.

The high-pitched whine started up again in the basement.

"Don't turn it on yet!" they heard Marigold yell.

"No, it has to go on now, because it has to interface with the polarizer!" Norton yelled back.

"No, it doesn't! That will create hyperbaric feedback!"

"No, it won't!"

"Of course it will! Where are your brains—in your big toe?"

"Look who's talking, dimbulb!"

"I know you are, but what am I? Ha, ha, ha!"
BANG!

There were two more loud bangs, and smoke began pouring up into the kitchen from the basement. Eddie and Marie jumped up and went over to the top of the stairs to see if their parents were alive.

"There it is. I told you. Hyperbaric feedback," coughed Marigold.

"Okay. What if we decrease the output?" Norton said, choking.

"Maybe," said Marigold. "We could try it."

Eddie and Marie could now hear them going back and forth, up and down the length of the basement. They were pacing together, coughing and walking. Eddie and Marie were used to this: first the insulting and arguing, then the pacing. Then it was usually back to arguing again. It was how Norton and Marigold worked. They'd never been any different, and they probably never would be.

The phone rang. Eddie answered it.

On the other end was the unmistakable voice of Oswald Regenbogen. "Hello," said the caller in his ridiculously nasal whine. "I believe there's a problem over there. I think I have a possible solution."

Oswald Regenbogen was definitely the smartest human being Marie and Eddie had ever met—except they hadn't actually met him. Nobody had. Ozzie was head of the Crisis Task Force of something called OOPS: the Organization of Practical Scientists. It was OOPS that gave out the Oopsie Award every year.

OOPS had about fifty members all over the country, and they were all very strange people. They spent large amounts of time in their basements or attics, inventing things like electric earscratchers and clocks that ran backward. The

Crisis Task Force was an important part of this organization, because OOPS members were often getting themselves into trouble—nearly blowing themselves up, turning large bodies of water to ice, or like Norton and Marigold Bicker, almost shrinking themselves out of existence. In fact, Ozzie had helped the Bickers out of quite a few scrapes in the past.

Ozzie, however, was incredibly shy, and almost never appeared in public. Nobody knew his phone number or address. He attended OOPS meetings by means of a special one-way telephone-and-television hookup that he had invented.

What Ozzie liked to do was think. He liked to solve problems. And if you got into some sort of big trouble, Ozzie simply called you. No one knew how he knew when to call; he just did.

"Young man," Ozzie said to Eddie, "would you please tell your parents to try recalculating the quadrilateral dipoles? That may just do the trick."

"Yes, sir, I will." Eddie tried not to smile when he heard Ozzie's funny voice. He always had the odd feeling that maybe Ozzie was playing a little trick on him, holding his nose when he talked on the phone.

"Goodbye, then," said Ozzie.

"Goodbye," said Eddie, and hung up. He rummaged around the kitchen drawer and wrote Ozzie's words down quickly, before he forgot.

"That guy is unbelievable," said Marie. "He kind of spooks me, you know? How did he know they needed him to call just then?"

"He's everywhere," said Eddie. "Like Obi-Wan Kenobi. I have to go downstairs and tell Mom and Dad what he said. Want to come with me and see what they're doing?"

"Not really," said Marie. "But I guess I will. Better to know what we're dealing with."

Waving their arms to dispel the billowing black smoke, the two of them picked their way down the rickety basement stairs. Basil followed them, almost tripping over his long basset-hound ears. At the bottom, a bare light bulb was struggling to illuminate the basement through the sooty gloom. Eddie and Marie had to wait for their eyes to adjust before they could see anything.

"Mom? Dad?" called Eddie.

"Over here," Norton called. "In the corner."

There, in the corner beside Norton and Marigold, was the time machine. It looked suspiciously like two rowing machines attached side by side, and it was covered with all kinds of equipment: belts, straps, wires, clocks, meters, blinking lights, whirring fans, something that bubbled, and many other nameless electronic doodads.

"Terrific," said Marie. "My parents, the time travelers." She could already see them arguing and pacing their way through the Middle Ages: a small woman with dark brown hair and a sharp, lively face, wearing fuzzy bedroom slippers, and a slight, balding man in wire-rim glasses and a tattered cardigan, marching up and down King Arthur's court before the astonished gaze of the knights of the Round Table. *If* her parents ever got there, which was doubtful.

"So," said Eddie, walking over to the machine, "this is it, huh?"

"This is it," said Marigold. "The crowning achievement of our careers. This one is really big. This one will make the world sit up and take notice. Thomas Edison, Albert Einstein, Marigold and Norton Bicker."

"Norton and Marigold Bicker," corrected Norton.

Marigold ignored him. "Do you want to know how it works, children?" she asked.

"Yes," said Eddie.

"No," said Marie.

"Good," said Marigold. "Here's how it works.

You know about waves—light waves and sound waves—don't you?"

"Sure," said Eddie.

"Well, your father and I were rummaging around in the fifth dimension, and—"

"The fifth dimension?" said Eddie. "What's that?"

"Hyper-time," said Norton.

"Hyper-time?" repeated Eddie. "What's *that?*"

"We don't know yet," said Norton.

"Anyway," continued Marigold, "your father and I believe that time has waves, just like light and sound. And we think that with our equipment, we can find the exact sound that those waves make. We call it the 'time hum.'"

"The 'time hum,'" said Eddie. "Hmmm."

"Not *hmmm,*" said Norton. *"Hum."*

"Now," continued Marigold, "if we can produce an audible time hum, that is, if we can make a time hum that can be heard, while we are strapped into our time machine over there"—she waved at the contraption—"then we're hoping that what we can do is sort of row on the waves of time. It would be a little like hanging onto a water-skiing rope, going up and down as you move ahead."

"Mom," said Marie, "those things are just

rowing machines. It'll never work. It's just too—well, too silly."

"People thought the fork was silly too," said Marigold severely.

"What about getting back?" Marie persisted. "What if you got stuck there? Or what if you went to sometime you didn't want to go, by mistake? What if it was dangerous there?"

"You're such a worrier," said Marigold, patting Marie on the arm. "You worry too much."

"Well, of course I worry," retorted Marie. "I don't think it's so strange to worry about your parents disappearing in the past, or the future, or who knows where."

"You know Ozzie Regenbogen would figure it out if something went wrong," said Norton as he tightened a toggle bolt on the time machine.

"Maybe," said Marie. "Even Ozzie isn't perfect."

"Oh, that reminds me," said Eddie, slapping his forehead. "He just called."

"Ozzie?" said Marigold.

"Ozzie."

"Unbelievable."

"Anyway, he said he thinks you should try—um—" He reached into his pocket, took out the pad, and squinted at it. "—Try recalculating the quadrilateral dipoles. I think that's right."

Norton and Marigold immediately began pacing.

"Quadrilateral dipoles," said Norton. "I never thought of that."

"Maybe we should make it $2x$ instead of $3x$," mused Marigold.

"Let's try it," Norton said, rolling up his sleeves and heading for the machine. "When is Ozzie ever wrong?"

"Children," said Marigold, "I want you to go upstairs. You never know what might happen."

"You mean, like maybe the basement might explode, and then the whole house would collapse on top of it?" suggested Marie. "Or is it that maybe we'll all take a trip to the Spanish Inquisition together?"

"No, dear, we're not going anywhere right now," explained Marigold. "We're just going to try to get the time hum right. If that works, your father and I will take our trip after lunch."

"Well, I'm really glad we're all going to have lunch together," said Marie as she and her brother went up the cellar stairs. Her sarcasm, she knew, would be lost on her parents.

"Maybe we should order out," said Eddie. "It's a special occasion."

# 3 PAST OR FUTURE?

Before lunch, there was a lot of noise from the basement, mostly humming sounds. There were little hums that went *bzzzzzzz*, there were deep booming hums that made your insides vibrate, and there was another hum like the one from that morning, which made all the spoons in the kitchen drawer bend into funny shapes.

Finally, Marie found herself drawn by anxiety to the top of the basement stairs. She stood in the doorway and listened to her parents working.

In a little while, Norton and Marigold started experimenting with the sounds of their own voices.

"Hmmmmmm," Norton would intone.

"Hmmmmmmmm," Marigold would chime in a little higher.

Then they'd be quiet for a moment, checking their dials and meters.

This went on for two hours. Finally, Marie gave up listening and helped Eddie get lunch ready. They had decided to cook something really special, since this might be their last lunch as a family. Eddie made canned cream of asparagus soup and chocolate pudding, his two favorite foods in the world. Marie cooked a tuna-noodle casserole, which was her favorite. Then she fashioned a little dog-food cake for Basil, decorated with tiny bits of muenster cheese.

The humming from downstairs went on as Marie crumbled potato chips over the top of the casserole and Eddie lit candles on the kitchen table.

"There," said Eddie. "You can't get much fancier than candles for lunch."

As they stood and admired the table set with paper plates, forks, and bent spoons, they noticed that the humming had taken on a different quality: Now it went up and down.

"Hmmmmmm," it went.

Then it went up and down even more: "Hmmmmmmmm."

"Look!" they heard Norton shout. "Look at the needle on the chronometer! It's moving a little!"

"Children!" screeched Marigold. "Come downstairs! Come and see! It's working!"

Norton whooped with joy as Eddie and Marie ran down the steps.

23

"Let's try a deeper wave, Marigold!" he said.

Norton and Marigold hummed again, in a slightly different harmony, going up and down even more. They hunched over the dial on the chronometer, concentrating. "Hmmmmmmmm," they hummed.

"YES!" yelled Norton "That's it!"

"We've done it! She's turning right over! Look at the potentiometer! It's going wild!" screamed Marigold. "Look!"

Eddie and Marie peered at the meter Marigold was pointing at. Sure enough, it was bouncing wildly near the top of the scale.

Norton and Marigold started dancing giddily around the basement. "We're going to travel in time!" their father yelled. "Yippee!"

"Yippee!" shouted their mother. "Norton, you're mashing my foot!"

"That's because you dance like a duck," said Norton.

"Let's all go upstairs and have lunch now," said Marigold, starting up the stairs.

"Okay," said Norton. "I'll be up in a minute. I just want to make sure the clocks on the machines are perfectly synchronized."

Marigold clomped upstairs. She was flushed and excited as she washed her hands at the kitchen sink. "We've done it!" she crowed. "We've accomplished something incredible, children!"

"Good," said Marie dispiritedly.

"Let's eat lunch," said Eddie. "You probably can't get cream of asparagus soup in ancient Greece."

When Norton came upstairs, they all sat down to eat, but the only one who actually got much down was Eddie. While Marie stared out the window and Norton and Marigold bounced in their seats, Eddie ate his tuna casserole.

"What will happen if you get broken, the way all the dishes did?" he asked conversationally.

"Eddie!" yelped Marie.

"Can't happen," said Norton. "There's kind of an invisible shield around you when you travel in time. It protects you and keeps you from changing. Everybody knows how it works with time travel—you emerge in a different time period, but you yourself are completely unchanged."

"H. G. Wells certainly knew it," added Marigold.

"That was *The Time Machine*. That was *fiction*," Marie protested.

"Who can say for sure?" said Marigold. "H. G. Wells was way ahead of his time."

Their conversation was interrupted by the sound of screaming coming from outside. Marie opened the curtains so they could see what the racket was.

Outside on the pavement in front of the house were Mildred Grackle and her boyfriend, Lenny the cop. Lenny was trying to reason with Mildred in his deep, slow voice, but he was having trouble being heard over the yelling of his beloved.

"You heel!" yelled Mildred, still hoarse from all the yelling she had done that morning. "You cad!"

"We didn't do anything," said Lenny. "We just went to the Law Enforcement Day picnic, that's all."

"Didn't do anything, my eye!" retorted Mildred. "I know what goes on at those things! A picnic blanket, a barbecued drumstick or two, and you lose your head!"

"But, Mildred, we didn't—"

"How *could* you?" moaned Mildred. "And with a meter maid, no less? It's humiliating! I had to find out about it from Imelda Krasnovsky. She saw you there."

"But Mildred," Lenny tried again. "It isn't anything serious with Martha. I just like her. As a friend. She wears the same shoe size as me. It's

26

nothing like what I have with you, pumpkin. You and I are—"

"Through!" shrieked Mildred. "You and I are through! I'm not your pumpkin anymore! Or your little radish flower! That—that meter maid can be your vegetable of the month now!"

And before the spellbound gaze of the entire Bicker family, Mildred turned on her heel, marched back into her own house, and slammed the door behind her.

Lenny stood on the sidewalk in the rain for a few moments, staring at Mildred's door. Then he shrugged his shoulders and shuffled off down the street.

"Whew!" said Eddie. "What did he ever see in her anyway?"

"Well," said Norton, standing up and rubbing his hands together, "I hate to eat and run, but I think it's time your mother and I were off."

Eddie blew out the candles. "Where are you going to go, anyway?" he asked. "In time, I mean."

"Well, we haven't really decided," said Marigold. "I think the Italian Renaissance would be nice."

"Don't be silly," said Norton. "We're going to the future. I thought we agreed on that."

"Well, I changed my mind," said Marigold. "I'm allowed to change my mind, and I want to go to the Italian Renaissance."

"We are going to the future," said Norton through his teeth.

"We're going to the Renaissance," said Marigold.

"Future," said Norton.

"Renaissance," said Marigold.

"Futurefuturefuturefuture!"

"RenaissanceRenaissanceRenaissanceRenaissance!"

"You guys are never going anywhere," said Eddie.

Norton headed for the basement door. "We will settle this downstairs," he said. "Come, Marigold."

The two of them disappeared. In a moment, the sounds of their bickering wafted up the stairs and into the kitchen, like a bad smell.

Eddie began clearing the table. "What do you want to bet they'll never get anywhere?" he said. "They'll never agree on where to go."

Marie was still sitting at the table, staring straight ahead. "I can't take this anymore," she said.

"Huh?" said Eddie, licking the last bit of chocolate pudding out of his paper bowl.

"I need stability," said Marie. "I need predict-
ability. I need order." She stood up. "I need new
parents."

As Eddie watched curiously, Marie crossed the
kitchen and picked up the phone book next to
the telephone. She began paging furiously through
it, looking for something. "Aha," she said at last.
Then she dug a pen and a pad out of the drawer
full of washers, screws, and computer parts that
was under the phone, and scribbled down a
number on the pad.

"Okay, Mr. Has-To-Have-It-His-Own-Way,
we'll flip a coin," they heard Marigold yell down
in the basement. "How about that?"

"Fine!" yelled Norton.

"Fine," said Marigold.

"Fine," said Norton.

They stood still in the kitchen until they heard
the slap of hand onto back of hand: the coin being flipped. Then there was silence for a moment.

"Okay," said Marigold.

"Okay," said Norton.

"Fine," said Marigold.

"Fine," said Norton.

"Where are they going?" whispered Eddie.
"Past or future? Can you tell?"

"No," whispered Marie. Without realizing it,

29

she was twisting the front of her sweatshirt into a small, damp knot.

In a moment, the rowing machines started up. *Whoosh, whoosh, whoosh, whoosh.*

"Time set?" called Norton.

"Check," said Marigold. "Clocks synchronized?"

"Check," responded Norton. "Straps tightened?"

"Check," said Marigold.

"Okay. Begin hum."

The humming began, over the noise of the rowing machines.

"Hmmmmmmmmmmmm," went Norton and Marigold in tuneless harmony. Louder and louder they hummed, faster and faster they rowed.

Eddie couldn't stand it anymore. He decided he'd go and watch from the top of the basement stairs. On the way, he passed Marie. She had written: "Acme Adoption Agency—555-6800," on the note pad.

"What's this?" he asked.

"What do you think it is?" Marie replied. "I'm going to offer myself up for adoption. Maybe somebody normal will take me home."

"I don't think a kid can—" Eddie began. But he stopped in the middle of his sentence.

All around them, everything had begun to hum. It was more of a feeling than a sound, but it was very deep. "Hmmmmmmmmmmmmmm," it went. It felt as if the whole house was humming.

Eddie reached for the wall to steady himself. It was vibrating. He looked at Marie, only to see two of her. In fact, everything in the kitchen seemed to have gone double.

"Eddie!" cried Marie. "There are two of you!"

"I know," said Eddie. "Like ghosts on the TV."

"What's happening to Mom and Dad?" Marie's voice was shrill with fear.

"I don't know!" said Eddie. "I'm going to go down and—"

But he did not finish his sentence, because the vibration had knocked him off his feet, and Marie saw two of him tumble headfirst down the stairs.

# 4 MILDRED'S WORLD

Next door, Mildred Grackle was sitting in her living room thinking about revenge. Revenge against Lenny. Revenge against Martha the meter maid. And revenge against Norton and Marigold Bicker, who were making her life miserable and were probably somehow responsible for Lenny's treachery.

Mildred's living room was a deep mustard color, with a kind of nasty olive-green trim. One wall was papered with Sunday funnies—colorful and economical, as Mildred liked to say. The coffee table in front of Mildred's couch was made of genuine coffee beans, all glued together with clear glue. Mildred was very proud of it; she had made it herself, and it was the only one like it in the world, she was sure. It was piled high with magazines: *Figurine Collector*, *Mushroom Growers' Monthly*, *True Stories of the Afterlife*, *Wrapping-Paper Swappers' Weekly*. Mildred Grackle was a woman of many interests.

Mildred threw aside the beanbag pillow into which she had been grinding her fist, got up, and walked through the wreckage of her china figurine collection into the kitchen to make herself a cup of tea.

To get across the kitchen, she had to push aside thousands of drying mushrooms, which were hanging from the rafters. This was Mildred's latest get-rich scheme: rare mushrooms. Her kitchen smelled rank, but she tried not to notice. Mushrooms were going to make her rich.

She opened the cabinet where the tea was kept, pushed aside her castanet collection, and surveyed the tea shelf. Mildred had teas for every possible purpose, concocted by a mysterious old woman who lived in the Bronx. She had Headache Tea, Bad Mood Tea, Good Mood Tea, Heartburn Tea, and Heartache Tea. She also had Revenge Tea, which was what Mildred reached for. But then she hesitated. Beside the Revenge Tea was an unopened packet of Love Tea. It was supposed to make you fall in love, and Mildred had never tried it because she had Lenny. (She didn't really *love* him, but he was good enough for general purposes. It was handy to have a policeman around.)

But now, Mildred thought, now she didn't have Lenny. She was a free woman again, and she could fall in love with anyone she pleased. And there would probably be a lot of people who wanted to love her right back. She was attractive, she thought, looking into the glass of the cabinet, and she was certainly interesting. The heck with Lenny! She brewed herself a cup of Love Tea.

While she waited for the tea to steep, she decided to haul out her Ouija board and ask it about her future. Many people thought Mildred's Ouija board was silly, but Mildred knew it was real. "My board is my best friend," she liked to tell Lenny. "It has never lied to me, and it never will."

The Ouija board was kept in a box, folded in half like a checkerboard. On it were all the letters of the alphabet, and the numbers 1 through 10. In the box, too, was a pointer that would slide around the board. You just had to put your fingers lightly on it, and it would seem to move by itself. ("It's not moving by itself," Lenny always used to say. "You're moving it." Mildred, however, knew better.)

Mildred set the board up on the kitchen table. "Okay," she said to herself. "Now we'll see what's what."

She closed her eyes, sat up straight, and took a deep, slow breath. Then she opened her eyes. "Wee-gee," she said, "you may be aware that my love life has taken a sudden and unexpected turn, involving one Martha, who is a meter maid. Was I right to give Lenny the gate?"

The pointer moved to the *Y* on the board, and then, as Mildred cackled gleefully, it moved faster and faster to the *E* and the *S*. Then it kept moving. *R-A-T*, it spelled.

"My thoughts exactly!" exclaimed Mildred. "You're so smart!" Then she thought of another question. "Wee-gee," she said, her voice dropping to a secretive level, "is there going to be another romance in my life soon?"

*T-O-D-A-Y*, spelled the Ouija board.

"Goodie!" squealed Mildred. "What's his name?"

The pointer seemed to be having a little difficulty deciding where to go. It went around in circles, finally pointed to *O*, then *Z*, and then careened crazily around the board again.

"Oz? What kind of a name is that?" wondered Mildred. "Where will I see him?"

*Y-O-U  W-I-L-L  N-O-T  S-E-E  H-I-M*, the board continued.

"Huh?" said Mildred. "What do you mean, I won't see him? How can I fall in love with him if I don't see him?"

*V-O-I-C-E*, said the board.

"I'm going to fall in love with his voice? What is this? I don't get it. Where am I going to hear this voice, anyway?"

*B-I-C-K-E-R,* spelled the Ouija.

Mildred jumped up from the table and slammed the board shut. "You are way off today," she grumbled. *"Way* off."

Mildred put her Ouija board away in disgust, and then sat down with her Love Tea. "Bicker, indeed," she said to herself, stirring in four table-spoons of sugar. "As if I were ever going to have anything to do with those people again in my *life.*"

She picked up the Love Tea. "Well, down the hatch," she said, and drank it down in one long gulp.

# 5 NERDS

The vibrating got a little better, and Marie was able to see straight again. She made her way uncertainly down the stairs, still unsure of her footing. At the bottom, Eddie was rubbing his head and trying to stand up. "I'm okay," he said. "Don't worry about me."

"They're dead this time," said Marie, trying to see her parents through the gloom in the basement. "They've exploded, I know it. I don't even want to look."

"Wait a second," said Eddie. "I don't think they exploded. I can see some movement." He squinted toward the rowing machines. A thick, smoky haze filled the basement.

The smoke began to clear, and Eddie and Marie were able to make out their parents. Norton and Marigold were still strapped into their twin rowing machines, coughing and waving their arms.

"Where are we?" choked Marigold.

"Is that you, Marigold?" said Norton. "What happened to you?" He peered through the haze at her.

"Mom, Dad, are you all right?" asked Eddie, rushing over to them. "Everything went double, and we—"

"Who are you?" asked Marigold. She turned to her husband. "Norton, who are they?"

Norton and Marigold looked Eddie and Marie up and down for a minute. Then they looked around the basement in obvious bewilderment. "Darned if I know," he said, shaking his head as he began undoing the straps on his machine.

Eddie and Marie looked at each other. "What's the matter with them?" Marie whispered into Eddie's ear.

"I don't know," Eddie whispered back. "The explosion must have confused them or something. Maybe they've lost their memories."

Norton approached them cautiously. "Who are you?" he asked.

"We're your children. Eddie and Marie," explained Marie.

Norton and Marigold both jumped visibly. "Children!" they cried.

Upstairs, the phone rang.

"I get it. They must be playing a joke on us," said Marigold.

The phone rang again.

"Maybe it's Ozzie Regenbogen," Marie whispered to Eddie. "If there was ever a time when we needed him, this is it."

Marie ran up the stairs three at a time. "Hello!" she yelled, grabbing the phone off the hook.

"You certainly do need a bit of help from me," said the familiar, nose-holding voice.

"Ozzie! I mean, Mr. Regenbogen! I mean, Dr. Regenbogen! Thank goodness you've called! Our parents seem to have had some kind of memory loss. They tried to travel in time, and they didn't go anywhere. Now they don't know us anymore."

"They've changed," said Ozzie.

"They have?"

"Yes. You see, ordinarily, when people travel in time, they emerge in a different era, but they themselves remain the same. Are you with me so far?"

"I'm with you," said Marie. But she was also thinking, *ordinarily?*

"Your parents, however, have done things backward. What I mean is, they have emerged in exactly the same time, but they themselves have changed. They've gone back into their own pasts. They're younger."

"They're younger? How much younger?"

"Probably about sixteen."

39

Marie sank down onto the chair beside the phone. "Oh, brother," she moaned.

"That's why they know each other, but they don't know you," Ozzie continued. "They knew each other for a long time before they were married, isn't that correct?"

"Yes," said Marie. "I think they actually lived next door to each other since the second grade." Marie closed her eyes. "So, let me make sure I understand this," she said. "Our parents look the same, but they're actually about sixteen inside?"

"That is correct," said Ozzie. "But there may be another problem."

"What's that?"

"The poof point," replied Ozzie.

"The poof point?"

"Yes. You see, your parents may not be done regressing. They may keep going backward in age, until they hit the age of zero."

"The poof point?"

"Yes. It's the point when they go so far back that they just go 'poof.'"

"I-yi-yi," said Marie. "This is just as bad as when they shrank."

"I'm going to try to help you reverse the process, but I don't know how long it will take me. There's a lot to figure out. In the meantime, they may be getting younger. And if they reach the poof point before I can help them—well, I have no idea what will happen."

"I-yi-yi-yi-yi."

"They could be in a certain amount of danger," said Ozzie calmly.

"Can I ask you a question?" said Marie. "If they do keep going backward, how fast will they go?"

"I have no idea," said Ozzie. "I have to hang up and call some other people now. They're about to melt Portland, Oregon, by accident. I'll call you soon. Goodbye."

And he hung up.

Marie stood there staring at the phone in her hand as if it were a smoking gun. Then she shook her head to clear it, hung up the phone, and went back downstairs.

Eddie was watching his parents as they examined all the equipment in the basement.

"Lookit," Norton said, elbowing Marigold in the ribs. "An oscilloscope."

"Neat!" said Marigold. She giggled.

"I don't know what this place is," said Norton, "but they sure have great stuff."

Norton picked up a glass vacuum tube from an old television. "Hey, lookit this," he said, handing it to Marigold.

The tube never quite made it into Marigold's

41

hands, however. It slipped and dropped to the floor, shattering.

"You dropped it," said Norton. "Butterfingers."

"I did not drop it," Marigold retorted. "You handed it to me wrong."

"I did not," said Norton. "Butterfingers, butterfingers, butterfingers."

"I'm rubber, you're glue, whatever you say bounces off me and sticks to you," Marigold chanted.

Marie, standing and watching this from the bottom of the stairs, caught Eddie's eye. "Psst," she said, beckoning him over.

Eddie walked over to Marie. "They're acting stupid," he said. "Was that Ozzie on the phone?"

In a hushed voice, Marie explained what Ozzie had said, as best she could. She saved the poof point till last.

"Don't worry about it," said Eddie. "I'm sure Ozzie will figure it all out before they reach zero. Maybe they won't even keep going backward at all."

On the other side of the basement, Norton was grinding the knuckle of his middle finger into the back of Marigold's head. "Noogies!" he yelled. "No backsies!"

"I'll get you back, Norton Bicker!" yelled

42

Marigold. She began chasing him around the basement.

"Oh, Lord," whispered Marie. "I really hope they don't go backward any further. Sixteen is bad enough. I hope I'm not that immature when I'm sixteen."

"They are kind of dumb, aren't they?" agreed Eddie.

"I just figured it out," said Marie. "You know what they are—I mean, were? Nerds. Science nerds. Our parents were science nerds. They were probably in the—like, the rocketry club or something."

They decided to go upstairs and think about all this for a few minutes. Maybe Ozzie would call back in the meantime.

They sat in the kitchen as they had earlier, listening to the sounds from downstairs. There was a lot of crashing and thumping, there were excited whoops as Norton and Marigold found more neat stuff in the basement, and there was arguing about whose turn it was to try things.

Finally, Eddie stood up. "Well, I'm going to walk the dog," he announced. "I can't just sit here all day. It's driving me crazy."

"Okay," said Marie. "Just don't take too long, in case anything weird happens."

Eddie hooked Basil up to his leash and left,

and Marie took a deck of cards out of the kitchen drawer and laid out a game of solitaire. It was something to do, at least.

She played a game. She lost. She played another game. She lost that one, too.

Halfway into the third game (which she was also losing), there was a lot of giggling in the basement, and then some electric-sounding snapping and popping noises.

"Catch it!" Marie heard Marigold cry.

There was a grunt and a flopping sound. "Missed it!" said Norton.

"It's getting away!" Marigold yelled. Then she began to giggle hysterically.

The hissing, snapping, and popping noise got louder, and Marie had the impression that it was coming up the basement stairs toward her. And then she saw what it was: a ball of crackling electricity, about a foot across, glowing like lightning and now bouncing along the kitchen floor toward her. Marie was horrified. It was moving quite fast.

Norton and Marigold came pelting up the stairs, jostling each other and giggling.

"Catch it!" ordered Marigold.

"You made it," countered Norton, making a face. "You catch it."

At that instant, the door opened and in walked Eddie and the dog. "Marie, you wouldn't believe what a beautiful day it—" he began, but stopped in mid-sentence as the lightning ball skittered toward him across the kitchen floor, darted between him and the surprised Basil, and escaped out the door, crackling loudly. It was headed across the double driveway toward Mildred Grackle's house.

Marie gasped.

Norton and Marigold clapped their hands over their mouths. "Uh-oh," said Marigold. "Who lives over there?"

"You don't want to know," Marie thought to herself.

And while she was thinking that thought, Mildred opened her kitchen door, carrying a basket of wash to hang outside, and the lightning ball scooted between her legs and into her house. Mildred dropped her wash basket and screamed loudly.

The lightning ball then emerged from the house and began to chase Mildred, who was still screaming. Up and down the yard they went, around and around the house. The thing was right on her heels; it seemed to have something against her personally. When Mildred zigged, it zigged.

When Mildred zagged, it zagged. Norton and Marigold watched all this with their hands still clapped over their mouths, spluttering with barely repressed giggles.

Finally, as Mildred ran down the driveway for the third time, she glanced at the Bickers' door. And she knew.

She streaked toward them, the lightning ball hot on her heels, ripped open the door without knocking, and ran into the kitchen. The lightning ball bounced all over the kitchen, buzzing and popping loudly, as Eddie, Marie, Norton, and Marigold ducked it.

"This is your doing, isn't it? Don't bother to deny it!" she said accusingly. "You made it follow me around, just to torture me." The ball settled down directly at her feet, like an electric puppy dog.

Marigold tried to keep a straight face. "We did make it," she confessed, "but we didn't ask it to follow you around. We don't even know you." And unable to contain herself any longer, she burst into laughter.

Mildred was so flummoxed, her mouth dropped open.

Then the phone rang. Eddie dived for it, carefully avoiding contact with the ball of electricity.

"Good afternoon," said Ozzie's nasal voice. "May I speak with your next-door neighbor, please? I think I can tell her how to deal with that bothersome object. It's attracted to her because she carries an extreme electrical charge."

Eddie held the phone out to Mildred Grackle. "It's for you," he said.

"What?" she said uncomprehendingly. Clearly, this was just another crazy event in the crazy house.

"It's a phone call for you," repeated Eddie.

With the ball dogging her footsteps, Mildred stepped over to the phone and picked it up gingerly. "Hello?" she said.

Eddie and Marie listened intently to Mildred's end of the conversation. What could Ozzie be telling her?

"Yes, that's me," she said. The ball sat at her feet, sizzling, as though waiting for her to get off the phone so it could start chasing her again.

"I should do what?" she asked.

"First I put the boots on?" she asked.

"All right, I understand," she said.

"What did you say your name was?" she asked.

"O-o-o-h," she said slowly. "I see."

"No, wait!" she said. "Don't go yet! Who are you? Where do you—"

But Ozzie had clearly rung off, and Mildred was left holding the phone, staring at it as though she had just heard a voice from heaven through it.

"Did he tell you what to do?" asked Eddie.

"Yes," said Mildred dreamily. "He's so smart."

"What are you supposed to do?" Eddie asked, not noticing this sudden change in his next-door neighbor.

"Oh, I'm supposed to put on some rubber boots, rub a comb on my sweater, and touch it to the ball of electricity," said Mildred, in the same dreamy voice. "Isn't that nice?"

Marie, who was a lot quicker on the uptake about these things than Eddie, was flabbergasted at the change in Mildred. She wondered if Ozzie had cast some kind of mysterious spell over her. But why on earth should he?

Little did Marie know about the powers of Ouija boards and Love Tea.

"Who *is* he?" Mildred asked, floating across the kitchen with the lightning ball right at her heels. She had completely forgotten to loathe her next-door neighbors. "Where does he live? How can I meet him?"

Even Eddie was noticing something unusual by now. "You can't meet him," he said. "Nobody can."

"But I must," protested Mildred dramatically, putting her wrist to her forehead. "I *must* meet him. He is my destiny."

He is a weirdo, thought Eddie. But then again, Mildred was a weirdo too. Maybe they'd actually be a good match. But Eddie didn't think so.

"His voice," rhapsodized Mildred. "It's so sweet! The way he talks—the way he says 'neutralize the implosive curvilinear negativity'—it's so beautiful, like the squeaks of lemmings in the mountains. And his name, just what my wee-gee board said. Ozzie." She said it slowly, as though she were uttering the loveliest word in the English language. "Ozzie—Say it loud and there's music playing. Say it soft and it's almost like—"

"Oh, please," groaned Eddie.

Meanwhile, the lightning ball was growing larger and louder, as if it were feeding off the energy of Mildred's newfound love. It gave a great pop, making everyone in the room jump, and edged itself closer to Mildred's leg.

"I think we'd better deal with that thing," said Marie. "Eddie, doesn't Dad have some galoshes in the closet?"

"I think so," he said. "I'll go look for them. What else do we need, a comb?"

"I'll go get mine," said Marie.

In a minute they were back.

"Here, put these on," said Eddie, offering the galoshes.

"Well, if Ozzie says so, I guess I should," said Mildred, her eyes sparkling. She looked down at her feet in the boots. "They do make my ankles look thinner," she said.

Marie handed her a comb, and she rubbed it vigorously over her sweater. It was so full of electricity, sparks jumped from it.

"Okay, now you're supposed to touch it to the ball," said Eddie.

"Here goes," said Mildred. She pointed the comb at the ball, closed her eyes, and jabbed it.

SSSPPFFT! The ball fizzed, spat, and disappeared.

"Wow," said Marigold from the corner.

"Cool," said Norton. "This guy really knows his electropositronics."

"I-yi-yi," said Marie.

# 6 GETTING YOUNGER

Norton and Marigold stayed sixteen for three days, until Wednesday. During this time, they installed an antenna for listening to cosmic noises outside the bedroom window; they performed an experiment on Basil, which turned his fur green; and they caused a ten-foot-high volcano to arise in Mildred's flower garden. Luckily, since Eddie and Marie were home from school on summer vacation, they could keep their science-nerd parents from doing too much damage. It was very stressful, however, and Ozzie wasn't calling with any help or explanations. On the bright side, Mildred never once came over to complain, the way she usually did; she was blinded by dazzling love.

Mildred had, in fact, taken to coming over to borrow things a lot—sugar, flour, a hammer, swizzle sticks. It was clear that she was hanging around the Bickers' house in the hope that Ozzie would call again. She also asked a lot of casual questions like "Where did you say he lived?" and "Is there a *Mrs*. Regenbogen?" Of course, Eddie and Marie couldn't provide any information about Oswald Regenbogen's personal life, and Norton and Marigold certainly couldn't, since they had never heard of him.

On the afternoon of the fourth day, Thursday, something peculiar happened. Eddie and Marie were sitting in the living room, reading, and their parents were in the kitchen taking apart the toaster. Suddenly, Norton and Marigold got the hiccups. Not only did they both get the hiccups at once, but they were really loud, major hiccups that jolted them from top to toe.

As Eddie and Marie watched, they tried everything: drinking water upside down, eating spoonsful of sugar, yelling "Boo!" at each other, holding their breath till they turned blue. But the hiccups went on and on, for more than an hour. The noise reverberated all over the house. "What should we do?" Marie asked Eddie. "Call their doctor? Call the pediatrician?"

"Let's wait a little while longer."

Finally, after almost two hours, the hiccups disappeared, just as inexplicably as they had come. One minute Norton and Marigold were hiccuping their brains out. The next minute everything was quiet.

They all looked at each other, hardly daring to believe that the hiccup storm was over.

"I feel funny," said Norton.

"I feel funny, too," said Marigold. She twisted a strand of her hair around her finger and changed feet. "Where are we?" she asked, looking around.

"Where's my mom?" asked Norton.

"Who are you?" Marigold asked Marie and Eddie. "Is this your house?"

Their two children looked at each other in complete confusion. What on earth could be going on now?

"I have to go," said Marigold. "Where's the bathroom?"

Suddenly, a light bulb went on in Eddie's head. He pulled Marie over so he could whisper into her ear. "I think I know what happened. They've just jumped back another level in time. They're younger now. That's why they don't know where they are again."

"So that's why they don't know us," said Marie. "I wonder how old they are this time."

"Let's ask them." Eddie looked at Norton. "How old are you?" he asked, feeling as weird as he had ever felt in his life.

Norton looked at him blankly. "Nine," he said. "Of course."

Marie turned to Marigold. "And how old are you?" she asked.

"Seven," said Marigold. "Do you know my

mom?" She was starting to look a little fretful. The stuck-out lower lip looked very strange indeed on a thirty-eight-year-old woman.

"Yes," said Marie haltingly, thinking about her grandma Edna, who now lived in Hawaii with her chihuahua, Edward. "I know her. She's very nice."

"I'm not supposed to talk to strangers," said Marigold.

This was a new problem. Eddie and Marie glanced at each other, unsure of what to do.

"That's a very good rule," Marie said at last. "You shouldn't talk to any *other* strangers. But we're not really strangers. We're kids too. And we know your mother. So as long as you're here, you might as well talk to us." It didn't sound that good. She didn't know if it would convince Marigold.

"Can I have a peanut butter sandwich?" asked Marigold.

"Whew," said Eddie.

"They're younger than us!" Marie whispered desperately into Eddie's ear. "I can't handle this!"

"You have to handle it," Eddie whispered back. "Until Ozzie calls, anyhow."

"Who are you, anyway?" asked Norton.

"We're your ch— We're Marie and Eddie," said

Marie. "You're staying at our house for a while, until we can—send you home. Okay?"

"Where will we sleep?" asked Marigold.

"You can—um—share the bedroom upstairs," said Marie. "It's very comfortable."

"Share a bedroom? With *him?*" screeched Marigold. "No way!"

"Okay, okay, we'll figure something else out," said Marie hurriedly. Even though her parents looked like her parents, Marie told herself, they really weren't. They were kids.

"I'll make you some peanut butter sandwiches," she said with a sigh. "Go into the living room, and I'll call you when they're ready."

Eddie helped her with the sandwiches. "This is funny, isn't it?" he said as he slathered a piece of white bread with strawberry jam.

"No, Eddie, this is not funny," said Marie. "Nobody should have to see what her mother was like when she was seven. It's not natural."

"I wonder if we'd like them, I mean as kids, if they weren't our parents," speculated Eddie.

"I can't even think about it," said Marie. "It's too bizarre. I think I'm going to have a nervous breakdown."

"I wonder if they're going to get any younger," said Eddie, licking the jam off his fingers.

Marie heard her teeth grinding together as she closed the peanut butter jar.

"Come and get it!" Eddie called into the living room.

After they had eaten, Norton and Marigold got up from the table. "What should we do?" asked Norton.

"Well," said Marie, "I guess you could read. Do you want some books?"

"I have books at my house," volunteered Marigold. "Should I go get them?"

"I'm afraid you can't go there," said Marie. "But we have a lot of books here. Do you want to look at them?"

"Sure," said Norton.

"Can I sit in your lap?" said Marigold. "My mother always lets me sit in her lap when she reads to me."

Marie almost choked. She could hear Eddie guffaw behind her. She had to admit, the thought of her mother trying to curl up in her lap was actually pretty funny. "Um—maybe tomorrow," she said.

They went into the living room and looked at the bookshelf that held Eddie and Marie's books. "I have better books at my house," said Norton.

"These will have to do," said Marie testily.

Norton picked out a book about Thomas Edison and sat down with it on the sofa.

Marigold picked up a biography of Marie Curie. "Who's this?" she asked Marie.

Marie stared at the book, and then stared at her mother. "She was a very great scientist," she finally said. "She discovered radium. I'm—I'm named after her."

"Neat," said Marigold. "I'll read that one. Maybe I'll be a scientist when I grow up."

"Weird," said Marie to herself.

Eddie and Marie left Norton and Marigold reading in the living room, and went upstairs.

Marie sat at her desk and chewed on her nails, trying to think of what to write in her diary. She hadn't opened it in a week, and she didn't know where to start now. She wondered what Eddie was doing in his room. She couldn't imagine that he'd be concentrating on much of anything, what with two children trapped in Norton and Marigold's bodies downstairs, but anything was possible. Maybe Eddie was doing just fine.

There was a loud noise from downstairs. "Hey!" Marigold yelled. "Give that back!"

Eddie and Marie rushed to the top of the stairs. "What's the matter?" called Marie.

"He took my book!" yelled Marigold.

"I was only looking at it!" Norton said.

"He won't give it back!"

"You wouldn't say please!"

Eddie and Marie looked at each other. This was too stupid for words.

Marie leaned over the stairs. "You two stop that, please," she yelled. "Norton, give Marigold her book back."

"Okay, okay," said Norton. "But she has to say please."

"Pleeeease," said Marigold in a drippy voice. "Now, give."

Norton gave the book back, and everybody settled down to their work again.

Five minutes later, there was a scream from Marigold.

Eddie and Marie rushed to the top of the stairs again. "What happened?" yelled Marie. "Are you okay?"

"He hit me!" yelled Marigold. "He hit me hard!"

He probably had hit her hard, too. He weighed 160 pounds.

"I only tapped her," Norton called. "It was an accident. She's a crybaby. And she tattles."

"It's going to be all black and blue!" Marigold caterwauled.

"I barely touched her!" said Norton. "Besides, she was bothering me! She was touching my knee with her foot!"

Marie went halfway down the stairs. "If you two don't stop it right now," she warned, "I'm going to have to separate you!"

"Okay, okay, we'll be good," said Norton.

"*I'll* be good," muttered Marigold. "*He* won't."

"Cut it out, Marigold!" said Eddie.

Marie looked at her watch. Six o'clock. They still had the whole evening to get through.

"I'll tell you what," she called down the stairs. "If you two can be quiet for a few minutes longer, we'll go to the movies, okay?"

"Goodie!" cried Marigold.

Eddie shot Marie a look. "Do you really think we should do that?" he asked quietly. "Can we take them outside?"

"We can't stay holed up in here forever," said Marie. "We'll all go nuts."

So, twenty minutes later, they were all on the bus, on their way to the Majestic Theater to see *It Came from Under the Sea*. For the whole trip, Norton kicked his foot against the bottom of the seat. His size-ten shoes made a lot of noise, and Eddie had to keep telling him to stop. Then Norton and Marigold had an argument about who was going to get to ring the bell. By the time they got off the bus, everyone on it was staring at them.

They got off right across the street from the movie theater. It was a wide, busy street.

Norton jumped off the curb, and Eddie just caught him before a car hit him. "Okay," said Eddie. "We're going to have to hold hands. Marigold, you hold Marie's hand."

They waited for the light to turn green. Marigold stuck her tongue out at Norton. "You were bad," she said. "Red light means stop."

Norton reached across Marie to try to hit Marigold.

"Cut it out!" said Marie, and smacked his hand. He pouted until they got to the other side of the street. Marie prayed they wouldn't run into anyone they knew.

"Is it going to be scary?" Marigold asked once they were on line.

"I hope not," said Marie. "If it is, we can go out in the lobby until the scary part is over."

"Can I get popcorn?" asked Norton.

"I guess so," said Marie. She had taken thirty dollars from the box she kept in her sock drawer; that had better be enough.

"Can I get Whoppers?" asked Marigold.

"Why not?" sighed Marie.

The people in front of them in line were trying very hard to not look at them.

When they got to the ticket window, Marie took out her money.

"How many, sir?" the woman behind the glass asked Norton through the microphone.

Norton just stared at her.

Marie jumped in. "Four. Children. I mean, two adults and two children. That's it, two adults and two children." Marie was flustered. By this time, she could hardly even figure out which two of them were supposed to be the adults.

There was a big line at the candy counter inside. The movie was starting in two minutes. "I want two kinds of candy," said Marigold loudly as they got to the head of the line. "Taffy Time and Coconut Chewies."

"We only have enough money for one kind," said Eddie. "Besides, it's not good for you."

"Pleeeease?" begged Marigold.

"We can't," said Eddie.

"Why not?"

"I just told you."

"But why can't I have two?"

"Because I said so!" said Eddie.

Marigold began to sniffle, and kept sniffling as

61

they went into the theater. People were starting to stare.

Finally, all the Bickers were settled in their seats, just as the previews were beginning. Eddie sat next to Marie.

"I can't believe I said that," he said into his sister's ear. "I always said that when I grew up and had kids I would never say 'Because I said so.' I'm not even a grownup yet and I said it."

"We were never as bad as they are," Marie whispered.

Norton and Marigold were both bouncing in their seats.

"Stop bouncing," said Marie.

A man in front of them turned around. "You're shaking my seat," he said to Eddie, assuming it was he who had done it.

"Sorry," said Eddie.

The movie started. A girl was baby-sitting in a quiet house by the seashore. She was reading a magazine.

"I'm scared," announced Marigold.

"Shhh!" someone scolded behind them.

"You're scared already?" whispered Marie.

"Yeah, I'm really scared! I want to leave!"

The man in front of them twisted around and whispered angrily to Marigold. "Can't you keep your children quiet?" he hissed.

Marie sighed and stood up. "I'll go and wait with Mom in the lobby," she whispered to Eddie. She and Marigold pushed their way out of the row.

Norton moved next to Eddie, and they watched as the baby-sitter turned on the radio and heard a report about a storm coming.

"I'm scared," said Norton.

"Nothing's happened yet," said Eddie.

There was a great crack of lightning on the movie screen. Norton tried to dive under his seat. He didn't fit.

"I'm scared!" he told Eddie at the top of his voice.

"SHHHHH!" said the person behind them.

"Okay," whispered Eddie. "We'll go, too. Get up, Norton."

They pushed their way out of the row and met Marie and Marigold in the lobby. Eddie looked at his watch. They had been in the movie theater for exactly seven minutes.

None of them said much on the bus going home. Marie stared miserably at her feet.

"Thirty bucks," she said.

"I know," said Eddie.

"That was baby-sitting money."

"We were never *this* bad," said Eddie. "Were we?"

# 1 MILDRED'S WORLD REVISITED

Mildred was packing. She had dragged her huge brown wicker suitcase down from the top of her hall closet, and was filling it with clothing. Her Ouija board sat open on the coffee-bean table.

"What do you think about the blue one, wee-gee?" she asked in her foghorn voice, holding a frilly dress up in front of her with one hand, while she kept the other on the board's pointer. "Will he like it?"

*N-O*, said the Ouija board.

"Okay," she said, flinging it aside. "Maybe something simpler."

She dug around in the back of her closet and came out with a tightfitting fire-engine red number, cut low in the back. "How about this?" she asked. "He'd have to be dead not to like this one, wouldn't he?"

*N-O*, responded the Ouija board.

Mildred was exasperated. "Well, what, then? What will make Oswald Regenbogen fall madly in love with me?"

*P-U-R-P-L-E*, said the Ouija. *H-E L-I-K-E-S P-U-R-P-L-E.*

"But I don't have anything purple!" wailed Mildred. "What will I do?"

Mildred sat down at her kitchen table to have a cup of Love Tea and think about this problem. She needed some purple clothes, that was certain. But money was tight, at least until her mushroom crop was ready. She couldn't go out and buy a whole new wardrobe in purple.

Then Mildred had an idea. She jumped up and ran to her junk box in the kitchen, where she kept all the things that didn't quite belong anywhere else. Aha! There they were, just as she remembered: two bottles of purple dye.

Two hours and one messy kitchen later, Mildred had a complete purple wardrobe: purple blouses, purple skirts, purple dresses, purple sneakers, purple underwear. The low-in-the-back red dress was now purple. So was the frilly blue one. She had even dyed her stockings purple.

"There!" she said, surveying her clothing with satisfaction. "Now he can't help but fall head-over-heels in love with me." She chose an outfit to wear for the start of her journey: a fuzzy purple sweater, a purple skirt with lace all around the bottom, purple sweat socks, and purple sneakers. Just lovely, she thought to herself as she looked in the mirror. She only wished she could get the rims of her glasses to be purple, but she didn't know how to do it. Well, maybe at some point she could add just a touch of purple color to her hair.

She crammed the rest of her clothing into her suitcase and sat on it so she could snap the latches closed. "Now," she said to herself bravely. "Now, all I have to do is find him."

Mildred reached into the pocket of her newly purple skirt and took out a wad of cash. This represented the total amount of money she'd been able to scrape up from all her little hiding places in the house, including her iron bunny rabbit doorstop, plus all the money she had in her bank account. Two hundred seventy-eight dollars and sixty-seven cents. Total. Well, if she took buses and slept in bus stations, she ought to be able to get far enough to find Ozzie. After she found him, life would take care of itself. She'd probably move right into his sweet little rose-covered cottage (after a small but beautiful wedding, of course) and begin her perfect life with Ozzie right away. Oh, it was all so wonderful!

Mildred put the Ouija board on her lap. "Now, wee-gee," she said, "how do I find him? Where should I go?"

At first the Ouija board seemed confused. It pointed to a few random letters, but didn't spell

much of anything but "pickle" and "mumps."
Then it got surer of itself. The pointer marched
around the board without hesitating.

*N-O-R-T-H-W-E-S-T,* it spelled.

"Hmmm. Northwest," mused Mildred. "Now,
what's northwest of Brooklyn?" Since Mildred
had never been out of Brooklyn in her life, she
had only a very shaky grasp of United States ge-
ography. Luckily, she had an old atlas on her
bookshelf. She opened it up on the kitchen table
and studied it. Then she closed it with a bang.

"Cleveland," she said. "Cleveland, Ohio. That's
our first stop, wee-gee."

Mildred folded up the Ouija board and put it
under her arm. Then she picked up her over-
stuffed suitcase, turned out the lights in her
kitchen, locked the door, and left.

In a moment, she was back in the kitchen. She
put down the suitcase and the Ouija board, went
to the kitchen cabinet, and took down the box
of Love Tea.

Mildred smiled to herself. "Mustn't forget this,"
she purred. "For Ozzie, my honey."

Then she turned out the lights again and set
out for the bus station.

# 8 THE LADY IN PINK

The next day, Friday, was a little quieter in the Bicker household.

Eddie had the idea of giving Norton and Marigold a deck of cards to play war, the game that never ends. It actually kept them busy for a couple of hours. Then he parked them in front of the television, where they stared blankly at cartoons.

"This house is a pigsty," said Marie to her brother. "Maybe we should clean up a little." Norton and Marigold had left socks, banana peels, and other junk all over the place.

"I was hoping I could go over to Lewis's house today," said Eddie. "We were going to work on our science fair project for next year. We have to start early. It's going to take a lot of planning." Lewis was Eddie's best friend.

Marie was terrified at the thought of being alone with her parents, but she knew this project was important to Eddie. "Help me clean up for a little while," she said. "Then you can go, okay?"

"Thanks," said Eddie. "You can always call me at Lewis's if you need help."

Eddie and Marie vacuumed, dusted, and picked up toys and clothing. Soon the place looked a lot better. They both knew it wouldn't stay that way for long, though. It was clearly impossible to get Norton and Marigold to pick up after themselves.

Eddie put on his sweater. "I'm only going for a couple of hours," he assured her. "If anything weird happens, call me up, okay?"

"Okay," said Marie, trying to ignore the feeling of sick dread in her stomach.

Eddie poked his head into the living room, where Norton and Marigold were still sitting on the floor, watching TV. "Bye," he said. "I'm leaving for a couple of hours. You guys listen to Marie, all right? Do just what she says."

He realized they hadn't heard him at all; they were in a television trance.

"BYE!" he yelled.

"Where are you going?" said Norton. "Can we come too?"

"No, you can't," said Eddie.

"Will you bring us a treat?" said Marigold.

"Maybe," said Eddie. "But you'll only get it if you're good." He had a couple of dollars in his pocket; it was worth spending some money on junk food for Norton and Marigold if it would help keep them in line.

After Eddie left, Marie sat at the kitchen table and played solitaire for a while. Then she decided to call her friend Lila. Lila was the most unfailingly cheerful person Marie knew. She could always make Marie feel better when she was depressed or anxious, which was very often, because of the fact that as far as Marie was concerned, she had been born into the wrong family.

"Marie!" said Lila when she heard her friend's voice. "Where on earth have you been all vacation? I tried to call you a couple of times, but your line was always busy. I even came by your house last night, but all the windows were dark. You must have been out with your parents."

"Yeah," said Marie glumly. "I was out with my parents."

"What did you do?"

"We went to the movies."

"Cool. What did you see?"

"*It Came from Under the Sea.*"

"I really want to see that. How was it?"

"I don't know. My—my mom got sick right after it started, so we had to leave."

"Bummer. Well, maybe you can go back and see it with me. You want to go today?"

"I can't. I have to, um, baby-sit." This conversation was not making Marie feel better at all. In fact, she was beginning to feel worse.

Marigold appeared in front of Marie. "Who are you talking to?" she asked.

"Nobody," said Marie. "Go and play. I'll talk to you when I'm off the phone."

"Can I have some bread and butter?" asked Marigold, continuing to ignore the fact that Marie was on the phone.

"Wait till I'm off the phone!" barked Marie.

"Marie, who was that?" asked Lila. "That sounded like your mother or something."

Marie panicked. She wasn't used to lying every two seconds. She wasn't good at it, and it made her really uncomfortable.

"It's just this little girl in my neighborhood," fumbled Marie. "She—she has an old voice."

"Wow, I'll say. Listen, guess what happened with Sean MacArthur today. I was in the park, just goofing around with Andrea and Michele, right? And we meet Sean, right? And Andrea and Michele start goofing around because they know I like Sean, right? Well, they sort of pushed us together, fooling around, and *he kissed me!* It was just a dumb little kiss, but . . . Marie, are you listening to me? I have the feeling you're not really there."

71

"Uh—I'm listening," said Marie. But actually, she wasn't listening at all. She was listening to some very strange and unsettling noises that were coming from the direction of . . . Oh, God, the roof! Marigold and Norton were on the roof! She could hear them scrambling around up there and giggling.

"Lila, I gotta go!" said Marie. "The, the, the kids are in trouble!" She slammed down the phone and sprinted for the stairs.

To get to the roof, you had to go up to the second floor, drag the ladder out of the closet, climb it, and open up a skylight in the hallway ceiling. This was not easy to do. But Norton and Marigold had done it, because there was the ladder, and there was the skylight, wide open. This was the worst of all possible worlds, thought Marie: seven-year-old minds in thirty-eight-year-old bodies.

She started up the ladder. "Oh, God—oh, God—oh, God," she chanted to herself. "Let them not fall off the roof."

She climbed up a few more rungs. "Wait a minute," she said to herself. "They can't fall off the roof. They have to grow up and have me. Right?" That reassured her for about a minute.

When she was about three quarters of the way

up, she could see Norton and Marigold on the roof. They were running around and giggling. She wished Eddie were there but she was afraid to take the time to call him.

Finally, she reached the top of the ladder. With a grunt, Marie hoisted herself up through the skylight.

She had never been out on the roof before. It was a flat expanse of tar with a tiny, low wall—only about a foot and a half high—around the edges. Marie had never thought of their house as very tall, but now she felt as if she were on top of the World Trade Center. The height was dizzying. She could see the whole neighborhood. Across the way, on the roof of Mildred's house, was a large mushroom-drying rack.

Norton and Marigold were busy playing tag. The television antenna was home base. They were careening back and forth, dangerously close to the edge.

"She's it! She's it!" yelled Norton when he spotted Marie.

Marie tried to control her terror and rage. "You," she said in a shaking voice, "will get down from the roof at once."

"Do we have to?" whined Marigold. "It's so much fun up here!"

"Don't argue with me!" snapped Marie. "Just do it! Now!"

"Okay, okay, okay," said Norton sulkily. The two of them made their way over to the skylight.

Marie took a peek over the edge of the roof. *Yikes!* The street was about a mile down! Marie felt some mysterious force trying to pull her over the edge. She jerked herself back quickly, panting, and ran for the skylight.

When she lowered herself through the opening, and felt around with her feet for the ladder, she found another surprise waiting for her. The ladder was gone. Norton and Marigold had removed it.

At that moment, the doorbell rang. As Marie hung helplessly from the skylight, she heard Norton and Marigold go pounding down the stairs, giggling.

"I'll get it!" shouted Norton.

"Me first!" Marigold rejoined.

"Get me down from here!" bellowed Marie. But nobody heard her.

Marie heard the front door being flung open, and then a woman's voice. Who could it be? What would Norton and Marigold do? What on earth would this person think?

"Marie!" screamed Marigold, thumping up the stairs. "It's for you!"

"Put the ladder back!" ordered Marie. "Quick. My arms are giving out."

"That was a funny trick, wasn't it?" snorted Marigold, dragging the ladder back into place beneath Marie.

"It was *not* a funny trick!" said Marie. "We'll deal with that later." She climbed down the ladder and rubbed her aching shoulder joints. "Who's at the door?"

"I dunno. A funny lady in a pink hat. Acme something-or-other."

Acme? "Oh, no!" thought Marie. "The adoption agency!"

Marie ran down the stairs, trying to straighten her hair as she went. She looked down. Her pants were covered with black soot from the roof. "Who would want to adopt me? I must look like a total mess," she fretted.

Downstairs, Norton was making interesting faces for the lady in the pink hat. It was amazing how ridiculous a grownup could look when his brain was nine.

The lady's polite smile was frozen on her face. Was that a glimmer of panic in her eyes? Marie thought so.

She took a deep breath and stuck out her hand in a hearty way. "I'm Marie Bicker," she said. "I called you." She pumped the lady's hand for a little too long.

"How do you do?" said the lady. "My name is Ms. Armbruster. We decided that I should make a home visit because your application was a bit . . . unusual. We don't usually get applications from children who want to adopt themselves out."

Norton was still dancing around in front of her. "Want to see a really good one?" he said. He pushed his nose up hard with one finger while pulling down his lower eyelids with two fingers from the other hand. The effect was totally disgusting, especially on someone his age.

Ms. Armbruster cleared her throat nervously. "These aren't—your parents, are they?" she asked Marie. "You didn't actually say if you had any parents, or what . . ." She backed away from Norton a little. Marie couldn't blame her.

"They're not my parents—exactly," said Marie. "They just live here. I kind of—take care of them. Do you want to go in the kitchen and have a cup of tea or something?"

Ms. Armbruster seemed grateful for the suggestion. "Yes, I'd love to," she said. "If it's not too much trouble."

"This way," said Marie. As Ms. Armbruster

walked into the kitchen, Marie hissed at Norton and Marigold, "Quiet! Or else!" Then she followed the woman into the kitchen.

Ms. Armbruster stood in the middle of the kitchen, looking around with her mouth slightly open. Suddenly, Marie saw the place in a whole new way, through the eyes of a stranger. It was an incredible mess. There were three rotting bananas on the counter. Beside them was a bowl of greenish goo, something Norton and Marigold had been fooling around with. Dirty dishes were everywhere, because Eddie and Marie hadn't had time to deal with them. Basil was lying on the floor, energetically chewing on one of Norton's slippers. And why hadn't Marie noticed that strange smell near the stove before?

"Now, dear," said the woman, carefully brushing the crumbs off the chair before she sat down at the kitchen table, "why exactly do you want to put yourself up for adoption?" She brushed off a little section of the table, removed her hat, and placed it on the table.

There was a crash from the living room. It sounded like the big lamp in the corner.

Marigold poked her head into the kitchen. "Norton did it," she said with satisfaction. "I didn't."

"Well, just play cards for a little while, would

you please?" Marie practically begged. "We'll look at the lamp later."

"Er—where exactly did you say your parents were?" asked Ms. Armbruster politely.

"They're away," said Marie, looking at her fingernails.

"I see," said the lady, looking as if she didn't see at all. And, of course, how could she?

"They'll be back sometime, I think," added Marie.

I hope, she thought.

"And why, exactly, did you want to put yourself up for adoption? Is it because your parents don't take care of you?"

Marie thought about it. Did Norton and Marigold take care of her when they were their regular selves?

They did take care of her, she thought—kind of, but not in the usual way. Norton and Marigold weren't big huggers. Sometimes they didn't come out of the basement for days at a time. They didn't cook regular meals or keep the house very clean or remember to send notes back to school. There wasn't usually even very much to eat in the house, unless Eddie or Marie bought it.

But, on the other hand . . . if you counted a birthday cake with little electric lights that ran around a "Happy Birthday, Marie" sign, flashing on and off in sequence, then maybe they did take care of her. And what about the long walks in the park while Norton explained the law of conservation of energy? Or the special midnight visit to the Museum of Science and Technology, with a personal tour from the director, who was a friend of Norton and Marigold's from OOPS? And what about her sixth-grade project, a working solar robot that Marigold had stayed up until two in the morning to help her finish? It was still on display in the lobby of P.S. 217, her old elementary school.

"Well, do they, dear?" Ms. Armbruster was asking.

"What?"

"Do they take care of you?"

"I guess they do," Marie replied. "I mean, they love me and everything. I'm sure they do. It's just that they're—they're not *normal.*"

Ms. Armbruster frowned deeply. "How do you mean, not normal? They don't harm you, do they? You can tell me, dear. You know, it's important to let a grownup know about these things. It shouldn't be a secret."

"Oh, no, no," Marie assured her. "They don't beat me. Nothing like that. They just aren't like regular parents. I want regular parents, that's all. Like on TV."

"Oh, I see, you mean parents like me, I suppose. I consider myself a fairly 'regular' parent to my little boy, Arnold." Ms. Armbruster smiled a smug little smile.

"Well, uh, what do you do?" Marie asked.

"Let's see," said Ms. Armbruster. "Every night, Arnold has a bath, and I check his ears and his fingernails. Cleanliness is very important, you know. Then I read him a nice uplifting story, one that will help him be a better human being. He always goes to bed at seven thirty-five, and not a minute later."

"How old is he?" asked Marie.

"Twelve," said Ms. Armbruster. "Like you, dear."

That was normal? Maybe she'd better reconsider, thought Marie. Who really knew what went on behind closed doors in other people's families? Maybe her own family wasn't so terrible after all.

Marigold appeared in the doorway again. "Norton has the hiccups," she announced. "He has them real bad."

*Uh-oh,* thought Marie.

Then Marigold began hiccuping. "Oh, no. I—

hic—have them, too," she said. "Did I catch them from Norton?"

"Um, I don't think so," said Marie, trying not to panic. But she was panicking nonetheless. Norton and Marigold were surely just about to regress down to another level, and the lady in the pink hat was there, and Eddie wasn't.

First she had to get rid of the lady. Who knew how long it would take Norton and Marigold to change this time? Or how old they would be when it was finished? In fact, who knew *anything*? Maybe Norton and Marigold would pass the poof point, zero years old, and then—well, who knew?

Marie stood up abruptly. "I'm sorry to have to cut this short," she said, "but I—" What? What could she say? "I need to think about this decision a little bit more." She stuck out her hand. "So thank you for coming, and goodbye."

Ms. Armbruster stood up, too. She looked from Marigold, who was still hiccuping in the doorway, to Marie, and back again. It seemed as if this was all just a little too much for her.

She shook Marie's hand firmly and put her pink hat back on, carefully brushing crumbs and dog hair off the jacket of her pink suit. "Well, then, dear, I guess I should be going."

"Yes," agreed Marie. "You should."

"Just call us if you feel you need any help." Ms. Armbruster glanced darkly in the direction of the living room, where Norton was hiccuping loudly and singing, "She'll Be Comin' Round the Mountain When She Comes."

"I will," said Marie, rushing her to the door. "Thanks for coming. Bye."

She just about slammed the door. Then she collapsed against it, trying to think what to do next.

Eddie! She had to call Eddie.

She ran to the phone and frantically thumbed through the family address book until she found the number she was looking for. Then she dialed, listening nervously to the constant hiccuping of her parents.

Lewis answered. "I don't know if Eddie can come to the phone now," he said. "He's right in the middle of something really delicate. It could mess up our whole project if he—"

"Lewis," interrupted Marie. "Get him *now*. Tell him—just say the word 'hiccups.' "

Eddie was on the phone in four seconds. "Hang on," he said. "I'm coming."

Maybe Eddie wasn't the most sensitive person on earth, but he was a lot more responsible than your average nine-year-old, thought Marie. She felt slightly better. Until she went into the living room. Norton and Marigold were unscrewing the base of the lamp that had fallen over.

"This is—hic—really neat inside," said Norton, sticking a screwdriver into its guts.

"Did you unplug it?" Marie asked in a panic.

"Nah," said Norton. "We—hic—we're being careful."

"Unplug it right this second!" ordered Marie. She was actually beginning to get used to dealing directly with the children who had taken over her parents' bodies. She hardly saw them as grownups any more.

"But why do we have to unplug it?" whined Norton. "We're being careful."

"Just do it!" Marie barked. "And don't whine!"

Marigold, hiccuping loudly, found the outlet and reluctantly unplugged the lamp.

Eddie burst in the front door, panting. He must have sprinted all the way home. "Did it happen yet?" he gasped.

"No," said Marie. "I don't think they're going to live that long. Either I'll kill them, or they'll kill themselves." Norton and Marigold hiccuped at the same time.

"I never should have left," said Eddie.

"No, it's okay. You needed to go to Lewis's.

83

But I am glad you're back." She gave him a big hug.

At that moment, they realized something: The room was quiet.

Norton and Marigold had stopped hiccuping.

# ⑨ NORTON TAKES A WALK

They all stood there. It was funny: even though Norton and Marigold looked exactly the same, Eddie and Marie could tell instantly that they had gotten younger. How much younger remained to be seen. But everything about them—the way they stood, the way they fidgeted, the expressions on their faces—was different now. Everything but their size.

Oh, where was Ozzie?

Eddie put his hand on Norton's shoulder. "Hi," he said. "How old are you?"

"Five," said Norton. "How old are you?"

"Nine," said Eddie.

Marigold pulled on Eddie's sleeve. "Where's my mommy?" she asked plaintively.

"Your mommy isn't here right now," he said. "My name is Eddie, and this is Marie, and we're going to take care of you until we can get you home, okay?"

Marigold stood there twisting the bottom of her shirt, and her eyes filled with tears. "Where's my mommy?" she wailed. If Norton was five, then she was three.

"Where's *my* mommy?" asked Norton. He looked at Marigold. "And who's *she?*"

Marie glanced at Eddie. "They're so young, they don't even know each other," she whispered.

"That's Marigold," said Eddie. "And your mommy isn't here right now either. But Marie and I will take good care of you, okay?"

Norton's face darkened. "That girl pushed me," he said, pointing to Marigold. "And I want my mom."

"I'll tell you what," said Marie brightly. "Why don't you two color for a while, and Eddie and I will make you some nice peanut butter sandwiches. And before you know it, we'll have you home. Okay?" She handed them some paper and crayons from the desk.

Norton and Marigold took the paper and just stood there.

"Right," said Marie, backing out of the room. "Sandwiches."

Marie smoothed the peanut butter onto the bread, and Eddie did the jelly. "Let's see," said Eddie. "Three and five. What are three- and five-year-olds like?"

"They can't read," said Marie. "We won't be able to give them books to keep them busy."

"Television," said Eddie. "That's the answer. I don't care if we ruin their minds."

86

"Good idea," said Marie. "Lots of television."

"Another thing we can do is—" began Eddie. But he was interrupted by Marigold, who had appeared in the doorway. She was sniffling.

"Where's my mommy?" she said. "And that boy—"

"Eddie was talking," said Marie. "It's not polite to interrupt. Wait till he finishes and then say 'Excuse me,' okay?"

"Another thing we could do is—" began Eddie again.

"But that boy—" Marigold interrupted again.

"*What?*" said Marie, exasperated.

"That boy went out," said Marigold, wiping her nose on her sleeve.

Eddie and Marie looked at each other.

"Went out where?" said Eddie.

"He went to look for his mommy."

"Uh-oh," said Eddie and Marie.

They ran into the living room, hoping Marigold had gotten it wrong. But she hadn't. Norton wasn't there.

Marie thought fast. "Listen, Eddie," she said. "I have to go find him. Can you stay here with Mom?"

*Mom.* It sounded *so* weird.

"Sure," said Eddie. "Go."

Marie threw on a sweater and ran out the door.

She looked up and down the street. Norton was already out of sight.

Marie thought about the options. If he walked a few blocks to the right, he'd be at a very big street, where the cars went fast and didn't slow down for anybody. If he went a few blocks to the left, he'd get to a scary, half-abandoned neighborhood of warehouses and boarded-up stores.

Marie tried to calm herself down. Norton would be okay, she reasoned. If he was getting into trouble, some nice grownup would help him cross the street or get back to his own neighborhood.

*What am I thinking?* she told herself sternly. He doesn't look like a five-year-old in trouble. He looks like a perfectly competent adult. Marie turned right and stepped up her pace.

What if I don't find him? she thought. Should I call the police? What will I tell them? That my father temporarily has the mind of a five-year-old? And at any moment he could get the hiccups and turn into a one-year-old? They'd probably cart *me* off to the loony bin.

She jogged along, looking down every alley, up every side street. Her heart thumped harder with every step. She kept thinking of more terrible things that could happen to Norton: He could get hit by a truck; he could get mugged; he could fall down and hurt himself.

She found herself remembering the time she had wandered off during an OOPS picnic up at Bear Mountain when she'd been four. By the time her parents had found her sitting by a lake and feeding the ducks her tuna fish sandwich, Norton and Marigold were so frantic they had alternately spanked her and hugged her for an hour. She distinctly remembered not having any idea what the big deal was, why they were so upset. *She* knew where she was the whole time. Now, as she walked up and down the streets searching desperately for Norton, Marie understood what her parents had gone through.

Marie looked down the street in horror. Ahead of her was Grand Army Plaza, a huge, complicated traffic circle with cars whipping around it at a frightening speed. What if he had wandered into that?

A truck rumbled by a couple of feet from her and she looked to her left, startled. When she did, she noticed, across the circle, the Brooklyn Public Library. It was an enormous building, with magnificent gold carvings on the front. As she looked at it, she remembered something her father's mother, Grandma Ernestine, had told her. "Norton," she'd said, "spent half his childhood in the public library. From the moment he could walk, he loved the books."

Maybe he was there! It was worth a try. Marie flew around the circle, crossing the streets that fed into it with reckless speed. She ran up the steps of the library and into the lobby. Two large staircases led to the upper floors. Where would he have gone?

The children's room?

She streaked across the lobby to her left, into the children's library. Oh, please let him be here!

At last she saw the librarian, at the far end of the reading room. She was bending over someone, probably helping a child decipher a word. Marie headed toward her.

And there, sitting in a tiny wooden chair at a tiny wooden table, was Norton, his knees up to his chin. The librarian was speaking softly to him, her face full of concern.

"Sir?" she was saying. "Can I help you? Do you feel all right? Is there a book you need?"

Norton wasn't answering. His lower lip was trembling.

"Shall I call an ambulance?" asked the librarian.

Marie ran over to her. "It's all right," she said. "He's my father."

Norton stared at Marie. He looked startled and confused.

"Is he all right?" asked the librarian. "He just came in and sat down, and he won't talk."

"He's—he's ill," said Marie. "Nothing serious. He just gets mixed up."

The librarian nodded knowingly. "Can you get him home by yourself?"

"I think so." Marie took Norton by the arm. "Come on, Dad," she said.

"I'm not your dad," he said. "I want my mommy."

Marie smiled weakly at the librarian, who looked embarrassed.

"We'll talk about it when we get home," said Marie, trying to pull Norton out of his chair.

"No," said Norton.

Then Marie had an idea. "We can call her on the phone when we get home," she said. "Yes! We can call up Grandma Ernestine, I mean, your mommy. She'll talk to you on the phone." Of course they could call her. She lived just a few miles away, in Queens.

"Okay," said Norton, getting up.

Marie thanked the librarian and hustled Norton out of the building.

They walked in silence for a few blocks. Then Norton reached out to hold Marie's hand.

Ack! Marie was dying from embarrassment. What if one of her friends saw them? What twelve-year-old walked around holding her father's hand?

Norton slowed down. "I was scared," he said.

All the embarrassment drained out of Marie in an instant. "I was scared too," she said, stopping and facing him. "I was really, really scared. You have to promise me that you'll never leave by yourself again."

"Why am I big?" he asked.

"It's—well, it's complicated," said Marie. "I can't really explain it. But you'll just have to put up with it for a little while, okay? We're going to make everything okay. And soon you can talk to your mommy."

Finally, they were home. They found Eddie on the sofa reading *Horton Hears a Who!* to Marigold, who was curled up against him, playing with a lock of her hair and sucking her thumb.

"You found him!" said Eddie, jumping to his feet. "Where was he?"

"At the library," said Marie, taking her sweater off. "We're going to call up his mommy."

Eddie looked at her blankly.

"Grandma Ernestine," she whispered. "Come in the kitchen with me."

"O-o-o-oh," said Eddie, getting it.

They walked into the kitchen. "What'll we tell her?" asked Eddie.

"Let's tell her the truth," said Marie. "She knows about the kind of stuff that happens around here. She's no dope. Besides, she raised him."

Marie dialed Grandma Ernestine's number, praying she'd be home. After about twenty rings, she finally answered.

"Hi, sweetheart," she said cheerfully when she heard her granddaughter's voice. "Sorry I took so long to answer. I was dyeing the cat blue. He looks fabulous."

Norton hadn't fallen too far from the tree in the Bicker family.

"Grandma, we have a problem," said Marie. "We need your help."

"Parents got a little carried away again?" asked her grandmother.

"Sort of," said Marie. She explained what had happened, which took some doing.

"Do you want me to come down there?" asked Grandma Ernestine.

"I don't know if you have to," said Marie. "Maybe you could just talk to him on the phone."

"Okay. Put him on."

Marie called Norton. He came into the kitchen, followed by Marigold, who was still sucking her thumb. "Your mommy's on the phone," said Marie to Norton. "You can talk to her."

Norton took the phone. "Mommy?" he said. He listened, and broke into a huge grin.

"Mommy! I miss you! Are you coming here to these people's house?"

He listened for a minute. "I will?" he said. "We will? Soon?"

He listened again, and then dropped his voice to a whisper. "What if they make me eat string beans?" he whispered.

Then he smiled. "Okay," he said. "I won't. Yes, I'll be a good boy. Bye, Mommy."

He hung up the phone. "Mommy says I should be good, and I'll see her soon," he told Eddie with a happy smile. "I feel all better. And you know what?"

"What?" said Eddie.

"I don't have to eat string beans."

"No problem," said Eddie.

"Can I call my mommy too?" asked Marigold, pulling on Marie's shirt. "I want to talk to my mommy."

Marie shrugged. "What the heck," she said. "Sure." Then she realized she'd have to explain the situation to Grandma Edna, too. "You go color for a couple of minutes while I get her on the phone," she told Marigold.

Marigold left with Norton, and Marie dialed her grandmother's number in Hawaii.

"Hello?" said a sleepy voice.

*Uh-oh,* thought Marie. *It's the middle of the night in Hawaii.*

Once her grandmother was awake enough to understand the bizarre facts Marie was relating to her, she snapped right into action. "Let me talk to Marigold," she said.

Marigold came to the phone. "Hi, Mommy," she said. "Yes. Yeah. But that boy was mean to me. Okay, I'll share. Do I have to share the red crayon too? Okay. Yes, they're nice. Can you come here soon? Okay."

She handed the phone back to Marie. "Thanks, Grandma," said Marie.

"They've really done it this time, the darned fools, haven't they?" said Grandma Edna. "They're lucky they didn't blow up the whole city. It's all Norton's fault, I'll bet. I told her not to marry him."

Marie held the phone away from her ear as her grandmother kept going on and on about Norton. She was used to hearing this from Grandma Edna. She just didn't need to hear it right now.

"Okay, Grandma. Thanks for helping. We'll call you when things are back to normal, all right? Bye."

Eddie was idly going through the stack of mail on the table. It was about a foot high, because nobody had been paying much attention to it since Norton and Marigold had started regressing.

"Hey, look at this," said Eddie, waving a piece of paper.

"Who's it from?" Marie asked.

"It's from OOPS. It's a reminder that Mom and Dad are supposed to be making their acceptance speech for the Oopsie Award."

"Oh, brother," said Marie. "When is it?"

"Tomorrow," said Eddie. "At the Waldorf-Astoria Hotel."

"You know how much they wanted to be there to accept that prize," said Marie sadly.

Marie raised her eyes to the heavens. "Ozzie Regenbogen!" she wailed. "Where are you?"

# 10 MILDRED HEADS WEST

Mildred and her Ouija board were on a bus to Phoenix, Arizona. They both looked a bit the worse for wear. Mildred's fuzzy purple sweater was pilling badly.

"Wee-gee," she said to her board, "we've been to Cleveland. We've been to Kankakee, Illinois, and Medicine Lodge, Kansas. We've even been to Leadville, Colorado. Our money is running out. I'm tired. Are you *sure* we're going in the right direction?"

*T-R-U-S-T M-E,* said the Ouija board.

"Is Phoenix really the place?" she said.

*Y-E-S,* said the Ouija.

Mildred just sighed, closed her eyes, and leaned against the grimy window.

An hour later, they pulled into Phoenix. Mildred rubbed her eyes and gathered her things together.

As she waited to get off the bus, the driver chatted with the woman ahead of her, who seemed to be a regular passenger. "Glad we got here safely, Gladys," said the driver to the woman.

"The weatherman predicted a freak hailstone this afternoon."

"A hailstorm, you mean, Bud?" asked Gladys.

"Nope. A hailstone. Just one—but it's supposed to be a biggie. Isn't that the darnedest thing?"

"Where will it all end?" said Gladys, shaking her head.

Mildred stepped off the bus, squinting in the gray light. "So this is Phoenix," she said to herself. She looked up at the great Southwestern sky.

Mildred was just barely aware of something rushing toward her out of the sky, something big and round and white. And that was the last thing she was aware of for a very long time.

When she woke up, she was lying on a stretcher. She opened her eyes slowly. Her head hurt. There was a bright light above her, and a lot of hustle and bustle all around her.

Someone in white leaned over her. "Where am I?" she asked.

"Phoenix General Hospital," said the person in white, who was undulating slowly.

"Hold still," said Mildred.

"I am holding still," said the nurse. "You've

98

had a bump on the head. Freak hailstone, apparently. You'd better lie still," he added.

Mildred closed her eyes and let her head sink back to the stretcher. At least she still had her Ouija board. She was clutching it to her stomach; although, why she still had any faith in it, she could not imagine. So far, it had led her not to Ozzie, but to a giant hailstone in a strange city. She lay there, feeling her head ache.

There was a small commotion near her. "But I just drove all the way from Tucson!" somebody was protesting loudly. "You have to let me go up and see him."

"Give me the name again," said another voice. "I'll check it one more time."

"It's Ozzie Regenbogen," said the agitated visitor. "Oswald J. Regenbogen. Room 522."

Mildred sat up like a shot. Ozzie! Her beloved!

"I'm sorry," said the nurse on duty. "Oswald J. Regenbogen, room 522, is not to be disturbed. No visitors."

"But I got some very important business with him!" said the man, who was large and unpleasant looking. "I gotta go up there!"

"If you keep this up," said the nurse primly, "I will have to call the authorities."

"Okay, okay, I'm going," said the man. "But I'll be back."

"Well!" said the nurse as he stormed out. "Some people."

The nice male nurse returned to Mildred. "Ah, you're sitting up," he said. "Are you feeling better?"

"Yes, I'm much—" began Mildred. Then her mind started clicking away. If she was a patient in the hospital, she'd be right near her darling Ozzie. And she'd be able to sneak into room 522 when things were quiet. Nobody would chase her away. Oh, she couldn't wait to see him!

Mildred put her hand to her forehead and groaned deeply. "I'm suddenly feeling awful," she said. "I don't think I can get up."

"Gee," said the nurse. "Maybe we'd better check you in for observation."

"Yes," Mildred agreed weakly. "Maybe you'd better check me in."

And so, Mildred, her Ouija board, and her Love Tea were checked into room 513 of Phoenix General Hospital.

That night at ten thirty, after visiting hours were over and the floor was quiet, Mildred stole out into the hallway. She looked both ways. The coast was clear. She pulled her purple kimono tighter around her and tiptoed in the direction of room 522.

There it was! Her heart was pounding even harder than her head, which was pounding quite hard.

She peeked around the doorway. There, lying in the bed, was a figure that was wrapped, mummylike, in white gauze from head to foot. There was a hole for the mouth, and two holes for the eyes, which were closed. Both arms and one leg were raised in the air, suspended by pulleys and ropes that hung from the ceiling.

"Ozzie!" whispered Mildred. "My darling, my own! What's happened to you?"

The man's eyes opened slightly and looked at Mildred in some alarm.

"Mmmm," he said.

"You don't have to talk now, my sweet," she said. "Just rest. I'm here now. I'll take care of you. I'm going to decorate your room all in purple. Every single thing. You're going to be so happy."

The man's eyes widened. "Mmmmm," he said.

Tenderly, she blew him a kiss. "I'll see you in the morning, my sugarplum," she said.

# 11  OOPS!

"We can't take them to accept the Oopsie Award," said Marie. "It's too impossible."

"You're right," agreed Eddie. "Too impossible."

"Let's call them and cancel," said Marie. "What's the name on that card they sent?"

"Hortense Schoops," Eddie read.

"Great," said Marie. "Hortense Schoops from OOPS."

They called Hortense and told her their parents had both suffered injuries in an experiment and wouldn't be able to come. "Could you just mail them their award?" asked Marie.

"Oh, dear, dear," clucked Hortense. "That really is too bad. You see, if they can't *receive* the award, we'll have to give it to someone else. OOPS rules, I'm afraid. Last year we had the same situation with Oscar Bunster. He was doing some kind of experiment with x-ray vision, and he got his eyes all crossed. He couldn't come, either, and he had to give up the award."

"Oh, this is terrible," said Marie. "The Oopsie

Award means so much to my parents. They've been hoping they'd win it for years and years, and they finally did."

"Gee, that really is a shame," said Hortense.

"Let me talk to my brother—I mean my parents—about it," said Marie. "I'll call you back in a few minutes."

She turned to Eddie. "They can't win the award if they can't show up to accept the award. OOPS rules. Hortense told me."

Eddie looked disgusted. "It figures they'd have weird rules. I guess we'll just have to skip the whole thing."

"But if Mom and Dad get back to their regular selves and find out they missed out on the Oopsie, they'll *kill* us. They want that award so bad."

"Okay," said Eddie with a sigh. "Maybe we can just take them over there quick, do the talking for them, and get out fast. I think that's the only way it has a chance of working."

"Okay," said Marie. "We'll try it. How bad could it be?"

Her question hung in the air. Neither one of them really wanted to answer it.

Marie called Hortense back and told her they'd all be coming.

And so, at two o'clock the next day, the Bicker family was on the subway to Manhattan.

"Let's practice again what we're going to do when we get to the big place with lots of people," said Eddie.

"We're going to be quiet," volunteered Norton.

"And not talk to any strangers," said Marigold.

"And Marie's going to take care of us while Eddie makes a speech," said Norton.

"And we won't bother Eddie while he's talking," said Marigold.

"And when we get home we can have ice cream," said Norton.

"Very good," said Marie. "And what will you do if somebody wants to shake your hand?"

"Shake hands like a big grownup but don't talk," recited Norton.

"Right," said Eddie.

Marie leaned over and said into his ear over the roar of the subway, "If we get through this, it will be a miracle."

"What?" said Eddie.

"Never mind," said Marie.

When they got to the Waldorf, the place was jumping. WELCOME OOPSTERS! said the huge banner strung across the lobby.

Eddie and Marie stood there trying to figure

out where they were supposed to go. They kept Norton and Marigold between them.

Up rushed a large woman in a blue flowered dress. "Norton! Marigold!" she gushed. "I'm so glad you could come!"

Norton and Marigold just stared at her with big eyes.

"Oh, I forgot—your daughter told me you weren't able to talk. Well, I certainly hope that clears up soon!" She turned to Marie. "You must be little Marie," she cooed. "I'm Hortense Schoops, dear. I'm so glad your parents decided to come. The Oopsie Awards Ceremony is so special. People just can't resist bringing their latest inventions to show off. I know you'll have a lot of fun today, children."

And off she rushed to kiss a man wearing a tinfoil helmet with a propeller on top.

Marie decided they'd better find the bathrooms before they went into the hall. Eddie spotted them across the lobby.

When they were halfway across, a man scooted over to them. There was something strange about the way he looked, but it took Marie a moment to figure out what it was: The man was severely cross-eyed. Oscar Bunster.

Oscar whooped for joy as he approached

Norton and Marigold. "OOPS handshake!" he cried. Then he raised his right knee, shot his right arm under it, and waggled his pinky at Norton.

Norton remembered his instructions from Eddie. He solemnly shook Oscar's hand, staring into Oscar's eyes.

"Gee, you must be working too hard," admonished Oscar. "Don't you remember how your part goes?" He demonstrated for Norton, turning around, bending over, putting his arms through his legs, and grabbing Norton's hand. "That's how you do it!" he said cheerfully. "Don't you remember?"

"Neat!" said Norton. He bent over, put his hands back between his legs, and shook hands with Oscar.

Marigold giggled.

"I guess you guys haven't seen me since I got my eyes crossed," said Oscar. "It took me a while to get used to it—I kept bumping into walls. But now I think I can see better than before. And wait till you see what I'm working on," Oscar continued. "It's wonderful. I just have to figure out what it's good for." He opened his jacket slightly to reveal a metal canister that looked like something from an army surplus store. "Don't tell anybody yet," he whispered, pointing at the canister. "Drooling gas."

106

He whipped his jacket closed again, and brought his voice back to normal. "Gotta go," he said. "See you later." And he rushed off to shake hands with someone else.

Finally, Eddie and Marie managed to get all the way to the bathrooms with their parents. They split up outside.

Five minutes later, they were together again.

"How'd it go?" said Marie to Eddie.

"Zipper stuck," said Eddie tersely.

A man came out of the men's room and shot Eddie and Norton a strange look.

"How'd it go with you?" Eddie asked Marie.

"Not bad," said Marie. "A little too much playing with the hand-drying machine, but otherwise fine."

"Let's go into the banquet hall," said Eddie. "The sooner we get this over with, the sooner we can leave."

"Right," said Marie.

She gave Norton and Marigold one final inspection. "You've been doing really well," she told them. "Just keep it up and we'll be okay, and then it will be ice cream time." She straightened Norton's collar, and in they went, marching resolutely across the lobby.

When they entered the hall, Norton and Marigold were greeted with a standing ovation, which didn't let up until all four of them were seated at the long table in the front of the room.

"Wow," Marie said under her breath to Eddie. "That Proton Enlarger must have really been a big thing."

"It sure was around *our* house," whispered Eddie.

Hortense Schoops, sitting at the end of the table, rose, cleared her throat, and adjusted her microphone.

"My dear fellow Oopsters," she said, smiling out over the crowded banquet hall. "I have the great pleasure of presenting to you the winners of this year's Oopsie Award for Excellence in Invention. Unfortunately, our dear Norton and Marigold Bicker are unable to talk at present, due to a small mishap in the course of one of their experiments. But luckily for us, they have brought their two wonderful children with them— Edison and Marie Curie Bicker. Edison has been kind enough to offer to give his parents' acceptance speech."

Eddie had not been listening to Hortense, as it happened. He had been trying to get Norton to stop sticking wads of bubble gum under the table.

"Psst—Eddie!" hissed Marie. "You're on!"

108

Eddie straightened up, flustered. He tapped the microphone at his place and cleared his throat.

"Um—ladies and gentlemen," he said, eyeing Norton nervously, "I'd like to thank you on my parents' behalf for this honor—" Marigold kicked her chair and began humming. She looked dangerously bored. Eddie knew he'd better wrap this up quick. "—And I know they would say thank you a lot better if they could. So—"

There was a loud clunk from somewhere in the audience, the sound of something large and metallic falling. "Uh-oh," said a voice loudly.

Oscar Bunster stood up. "Sorry to tell you this, everyone," he said. "And I'm sorry to interrupt your speech," he added, waving weakly at Eddie. "But I've just dropped my canister of drooling gas, and it's sort of ruptured. I'm afraid you'll all be beginning to drool in a few seconds. But don't worry. It only lasts for an hour."

The room was silent, except for a loud *pffft* sound—gas leaking from Oscar's canister. As it filled the room, smelling a little like pineapple, there was more exasperation than shock on the faces in the audience. OOPS people were used to their own experiments going haywire, but they didn't expect to have to put up with other people's mishaps.

"Darn it, Oscar, why didn't you leave that fool thing at home?" said somebody.

The pineapple smell grew stronger, and then the drooling began. Drool dripped from every mouth in the room—onto plates, onto the floor, onto shoes. The gas seemed to have the additional effect of putting people into a kind of stupor, so everybody just sat and stared and drooled. It was nauseating.

For some reason, probably having to do with their already altered state, Norton and Marigold were unaffected by the drooling gas. The two of them giggled and poked one another and pointed at the helpless, drooling grownups. "They're funny!" crowed Marigold.

Eddie and Marie, who were drooling and staring just like everyone else, were fighting to overcome the near-paralysis that had come over them. Even though their bodies had lost control, their minds were still working well enough to know that a disaster was in the making here.

Norton discovered that it was fun to hop across the carpeted floor.

"Marie," drooled Eddie, "Marie, we have got to get out of here."

"Uuuuhh," was the best Marie could do.

Norton had now grabbed Marigold's hand, and the two of them were hopping back and forth across the ballroom.

"Marie," Eddie slobbered, "let'sh go!" By a supreme effort of will, he moved his hand over to his sister's wrist and clamped on.

"Uurgh," bubbled Marie. Eddie could see that she was fighting hard to get some control.

"Look! We're hopping!" shouted Norton, just before he hurtled into a table that held a huge bowl of punch and about a hundred glass cups. The punch bowl teetered in slow motion, gave up trying, and crashed to the floor, accompanied by all the cups.

"One . . . two . . . three," mumbled Eddie with tremendous concentration. "Shtand up."

Marie was working so hard to overcome the stupor that accompanied the drooling that her eyes almost crossed. She drooled even harder with the effort. Hanging onto Eddie, she stood up shakily.

Inch by inch, they made their way across the floor. It was so hard to think! All they wanted to do was sit down on the floor and stare. And drool. But they had to go on.

Norton and Marigold were now hopping around each table. All of OOPS was sitting

111

transfixed, staring at them. Their fronts were covered with drool. Oscar Bunster was going to be in some very deep trouble when his gas wore off, that was for sure.

Finally, after about fifteen minutes, Eddie and Marie had reached the door. Their muscles felt like mush.

"Nor . . ." he slurred. "Marrggle . . . Time to go. Shay g'bye."

"But why?" whined Marigold. "This is fun!"

Marie leaned against the door and gathered her strength. Finally, with a gigantic effort, she managed to drag one word from deep inside herself. "NOW!" she gargled. Then she collapsed against Eddie.

Little kids can always tell when somebody is really, truly serious, and Norton and Marigold were no exception. Recognizing genuine fury in Marie's tone of voice, they stopped in mid-hop and ran to the door.

"Bye!" called Marigold, waving to the staring, drooling group. Nobody responded.

"Thank you!" added Norton politely.

And then, finally, they were out on the street. As soon as they hit the fresh air, Eddie and Marie felt better. They sat down on the curb to rest, not caring what the throngs of passersby thought.

And no one even noticed the two panting, drool-covered kids, or the two grownups who were jumping from box to box on the sidewalk near them. New Yorkers were used to anything.

# 12 MILDRED GRACKLE, GUN MOLL

Oswald J. Regenbogen's room was now decorated completely in purple. There were purple vases full of purple flowers on every flat surface. There was shiny purple fabric draped over the chair, hung over the end of the bed, and festooning the window. And there was a large, unframed poster hanging on the wall above the bed, titled "Purple Dawn."

Mildred surveyed her handiwork. "Here," she said. "It's as purple as I can make it for the time being." She turned to the mummy in the bed. "What do you think, snookums?" she asked the mummy.

The figure rolled its eyes. An untouched cup of Love Tea sat on the bedside table.

"I know it's not fabulous, my little pumpernickel," she fretted, "but it's the best I can do on such short notice. I'm sure that where *you* live, it's very different. I'm sure it's just a—a—purple fantasy!" She laughed a tinkly laugh, delighted with her little turn of phrase.

"Now," she said brightly, approaching the bed. "Let's make you all nice and comfy. Maybe we

114

should lower that leg just a teensy bit so it doesn't have to be hanging all the way up in the air like that."

A look of sheer terror flashed in the mummy's eyes. It began hyperventilating.

"Ahem."

There was a man standing in the doorway. He needed a shave. He was large.

"This is Regenbogen's room, right?" This was a man without a shred of charm. Mildred disapproved. Whoever he was, he certainly wasn't going to be allowed to annoy her Oswald.

"You are correct," she snapped. "But he is resting at the moment. He can't be disturbed. Please come back another day."

"Get lost, sister."

Mildred was so shocked, she reverted back to her old self. "Listen, bub," she said in her normal meat-grinder voice, "there's only one person here that's leaving, and it's not me and it's not him. It's you. You think you can talk to me like that, you have another think coming. Beat it."

The man was beginning to get annoyed. He held up the folded newspaper he was carrying, just enough so that Mildred could get a glimpse of the shiny black metal object that was tucked into it. It was definitely a gun.

"Now, I'm only going to say this once," he

115

snarled. "Me and him got some business to talk about. Private business. See, I'm a friend of his. But there's some people that aren't. He already had one 'accident,' owing to a not very good business deal he made. I'm trying to help him out here, before they come back and give him another accident. I don't know who you are, but I know he never liked no women around complicating up his life. So would you please get lost here, please?"

Mildred was trying to absorb this information. "Oswald, is this true?" she demanded of the mummy. "Is this man your friend? Blink once if it's yes, and twice if it's no."

The man blinked once.

"Should I go?" she said.

One blink.

"Because I can stay. If you need me, I really could stay, and I could—" But he was blinking and blinking. The message was clear. She should go.

"Well, then," she said uncertainly, "if you really think it's okay—"

"Would you go, lady?" roared the big man.

A small man in a black suit and a pink tie materialized in the door. "Trouble, Manny?" he asked.

116

"Nah. It's okay. I got it under control."

"Is she bothering the boss?" asked the small man, glancing at the mummy.

"She was just leaving," said the big guy.

Mildred gathered up her purple cloth with as much dignity as she could muster. "I'll be going now," she said. "And you should learn how to talk to a lady, *buster*."

With a backward look at the man in the bed, she pushed past the small man in the doorway.

Back in her own room, she collapsed on the bed. The Ouija board lay open beside her.

"Oh, wee-gee, wee-gee," she moaned, "this is all so *strange!*" She sat up suddenly and put the board on her lap. "I need some answers," she muttered.

She put her fingers on the pointer and took a breath. "Was I right to leave?" she asked.

*Y-E-S*, said the Ouija.

"Were those men going to hurt him?"

*N-O. T-H-E-Y W-O-R-K F-O-R H-I-M.* The pointer was really flying around the board.

Mildred bit her lip. "What business, exactly, is Oswald J. Regenbogen *in?*" she asked.

*N-U-M-B-E-R-S. L-O-A-N-S-H-A-R-K-I-N-G. R-A-C-K-E-T-S.*

Mildred gasped. "You mean, he's a gangster?"

*Y-E-S-Y-E-S-Y-E-S-Y-E-S-Y-E-S,* chattered the board.

Mildred jumped up, and the Ouija board went clattering to the floor. "I *knew* it!" she screeched. "I *knew* something was wrong. How could I be so blind? How could I fall in love with a *criminal?*"

She stomped around the room, throwing her things into her suitcase. She slammed it shut, paced a bit, then opened it up and took out every purple item in it. Then she slammed it shut again. "Goodbye, Phoenix," she muttered.

Then she decided she would just take herself down to Oswald's room and give him a piece of her mind. How dare he lead her on like that?

The door of room 522 was just slightly ajar. She pushed it open. The bed was unoccupied and the traction rings were hanging empty. Oswald J. Regenbogen had taken a powder, flown the coop, scrammed.

Mildred stomped back to her room, sat down at the phone, and dialed.

"Hello?" said a voice.

"Who is this?" demanded Mildred.

"Marie Bicker. Who is *this?*"

"This is your next-door neighbor, Mildred Grackle. I want you to know that I've found your friend Oswald J. Regenbogen, and he's *very sick.*"

118

"You found him? But where—"

"And I also want you to know that you and your family are responsible for every single bad thing that has ever happened to me in my entire life!" Mildred slammed the phone down.

Then she picked up the phone again and dialed another number.

"Hello?" said another voice.

"Lenny?" said Mildred.

"Mildred?" said Lenny.

"Lenny, I want you to know that I forgive you. All—all is forgiven. I'm coming home. To you."

"But—"

Mildred hung up, smiling. She would put the pieces of her life back together. She was a survivor.

She took a last look around her hospital room. Everything she needed was packed. Her purple sweater was in a ball on the floor. On the way out, she had to pass room 522. She couldn't resist walking in one more time, just to stand there and look around. She stood at the foot of the bed, staring bitterly at the place where Oswald J. Regenbogen, hardened criminal, had lain.

What was this? Something green was sticking out from under the mattress. A piece of paper. The color of money.

She pulled it out. It was a five-hundred-dollar bill.

As Mildred marched down the hall past the nurses' station toward the elevator, a voice called out to her.

"Wait!" cried the nurse. "You can't just leave! You have a head injury, and we have to observe you, and—"

"Forget it, honey," said Mildred as the elevator doors closed.

She walked out of the hospital and got into a taxi. "Take me to the airport," she said. "And step on it."

# 13 STRETCHING THE SPACE-TIME FABRIC

As soon as Marie and Eddie walked in the door, still sticky with drool but more or less recovered, the phone rang. Marie ran into the kitchen to get it, praying it was Ozzie.

Two minutes later, she was back in the living room. She didn't look good.

"Marie, you look freaked out," said Eddie. "Who was on the phone? Was it Ozzie?"

Norton and Marigold were sitting in the corner on the floor, inspecting each other's feet. They had begun hiccuping during the subway ride home from the Waldorf-Astoria, and this time they had not stopped. They seemed to be regressing steadily, but it was impossible to tell how far or how fast.

"It wasn't Ozzie, it was Mildred Grackle," said Marie. "She said she's found Ozzie, and he's very sick. Then she hung up." Marie's throat tightened and tears welled up in her eyes.

"But he can't be sick!" said Eddie. "He's our only hope!"

"He must be really sick," said Marie. "That's

121

probably why he hasn't called." She was crying hard now. She couldn't help it.

Eddie started crying too. Eddie never cried. "What's going to happen to them?" he sniffled. "They're going to poof pretty soon and—"

The phone rang.

"It's probably Mildred again," said Marie, wiping her eyes. "She probably wants to tell us some curses she forgot."

She shuffled to the phone, trying to get a grip on herself, trying not to let the constant hiccuping make her feel crazy. She would just tell Mildred, she decided, that she should take her bad temper somewhere else. The Bickers had bigger problems.

"Hello?" she said, wiping her nose with the back of her hand.

"Hello," said a funny, nasal voice. "Regenbogen here."

"Ozzie? I mean, Dr. Regenbogen? Is it really you?"

"None other," said Ozzie.

"But, are you okay? Are you sick?"

Ozzie chuckled, a small, whining sound. "Heard that from Mildred Grackle, did you?"

"Yes," said Marie, flabbergasted as always by the extent of his knowledge. "But how did you—"

122

"I've been keeping tabs on her. Didn't want her to get too close."

"She said she found you."

"She found Oswald *J.* Regenbogen. Distant cousin of mine. Mobster—black sheep of the family. I'm Oswald *P.* Regenbogen."

"You mean," said Marie, "she found the wrong Ozzie Regenbogen?"

"Precisely," said Ozzie. "Now, we have things to talk about. Your parents will be reaching the poof point quite soon."

"I know," said Marie. "Where have you been? We're going nuts here."

"Didn't call because I didn't have anything to say. I still don't know what's going to happen. But I figured I should be on the line when they get to the poof point. What are they doing right now?"

Marie put her hand over the phone. "Eddie!" she called. "What are they doing right now?"

"Lying on their backs and hiccuping," Eddie yelled back. "Norton's playing with his toes. Is that Ozzie on the phone?"

"Yes!"

"Thank God!"

Marie reported Norton and Marigold's condition to Ozzie.

"As I thought," mused Ozzie. "Norton is two years older than Marigold, correct?"

"Yes."

"At this accelerated pace, your mother will probably poof about fifteen seconds before your father."

"What do you think might happen?" asked Marie.

"We-e-ell," said Ozzie thoughtfully, "most people think of the space-time fabric as being rather stiff and inflexible, like—er, perhaps new denim."

"They do?"

"But I prefer to think of it as being more stretchy and elastic—like spandex, perhaps."

"So, what does that mean?"

"It means, my dear girl, that your parents might just make it through the poof point. Of course, there will probably be quite a bit of vibration. And then again, they might not make it through at all."

"Oh," said Marie.

Immediately, a peculiar feeling began going through Marie's body. Everything was vibrating, very much the way it had when her parents had had their first disaster with the time machine.

"Uh-oh," she said, fighting hysteria. "Something big is happening. Here we go."

Eddie came pelting into the room. "What's going on?"

"Hang on," said Ozzie into the phone. "The next couple of minutes may be a bit rough."

"Eddie!" yelled Marie. "Go back in the living room and watch Mom and Dad. Make sure they don't disappear or explode or something. I'll stay on the phone with Ozzie."

"Got it," said Eddie, and ran back to the living room. "They look okay!" he shouted back. "They're still hiccuping!"

The vibrating got worse. Basil came running into the kitchen with his tail between his legs and his ears down. Marie felt her teeth shaking in her head. She could hardly see, because her eyeballs were vibrating.

"What's happening?" she called in to Eddie.

"They're still here," Eddie yelled back. "But they're both whimpering. They seem to be in pain!"

"Here it comes," said Ozzie.

"Here it comes!" yelled Marie to Eddie.

There was a loud noise that filled the house: THWUMP! Then there was a noise that sounded like an unthinkably huge piece of elastic being twanged: BOYOYOYOYOING!

Abruptly, the vibrating stopped and there was an odd, almost dead peace.

Then Eddie yelled, "Mom sat up! She's rubbing her eyes!"

"That was number one," said Ozzie to a startled Marie, who had forgotten she was holding the phone to her ear. "We still have number two to go."

The vibrating immediately started up again—just a little at first, then building to the same tooth-rattling shaking that had happened just a minute ago. It seemed to last a bit longer this time, and took on a strangely dreamlike quality. Marie stood rooted to the floor.

BOYOYOYOYOYOING!

Again, there was a stillness in the house.

"Dad is sitting up too!" Eddie shrieked. "They're okay!"

"Well," said Ozzie, "they seem to have passed the poof point in one piece. We'll have to see what's actually happened."

Marie stretched the phone cord as far as it could go, and found that she could just see into the living room while talking to Ozzie.

"See if they can talk," suggested Ozzie.

Marie looked at her mother and father. Of the two, Marigold seemed to be more fully recovered from the poofing experience. She was standing up now, brushing off her clothes and looking around.

"Hello?" said Marie tentatively.

"Hello?" said Marigold in an extremely bewildered tone of voice. "Where am I?"

"In your living room," said Marie gently.

"Where's my plane?" said Marigold, looking a bit wild-eyed now. *"Where's my airplane?"*

Marie became aware of Ozzie's voice in her ear. "Just as I'd suspected," he said. "Ask her what her name is."

"What?"

"Go on, just ask her."

Marie cleared her throat. "Excuse me . . . can I ask what your name is?"

Eddie was staring at everyone.

"Why, it's Amelia," said Marigold. "Amelia Earhart."

Marie dropped the phone.

"But—but," yammered Eddie. "Amelia Earhart disappeared at sea. A long time ago. She's, well, you know, dead, right?"

Oswald's tiny voice emanated from the phone. "Hello? Hello? Pick up the phone, please!" Marie bent down and picked it up. "This is just what I thought might happen," said Ozzie. "They've poofed back beyond zero into a past life. Amelia Earhart's plane was lost in 1937, when she was trying to be the first woman to fly around the world. She certainly died when her plane went down. I think your mother was Amelia Earhart before she was Marigold Bicker."

"Holy cow," said Marie.

"What's happening?" Eddie asked desperately. "What's Ozzie saying?"

"Past lives," whispered Marie. "They've poofed into past lives."

"Oh," said Eddie.

"Talk to your father—see what he says," suggested Ozzie.

Marie looked at her father. He was just getting to his feet.

# 14 POOFING AND POOFING

Marigold was still staring around the room in confusion. Norton's expression was confused, too, but also angry—his eyebrows were lowered in a scowl, and his jaw was thrust out pugnaciously. He stood surveying the room with his arms akimbo.

"Hello," said Marie cautiously. "Who are you?"

"Who wants to know?" he countered.

"We won't hurt you," said Eddie.

"You mugs better not try anything," rasped Norton in a gruff voice that sounded completely ridiculous coming from him. "My name's Bugsy. Bugsy Berkowitz. Don't mess with me." He squinted through his glasses as he said it.

Bugsy? thought Marie. Like a gangster? This was unreal.

"Er—hi, Mr. Berkowitz. Welcome to our home. I'm Marie, and this is Eddie, and this is—um—this is Amelia Earhart."

"*The* Amelia Earhart?" said Bugsy/Norton, impressed.

"I suppose so," said Amelia/Marigold modestly. "I mean, I think there's only one of me."

"Aren't you getting ready to fly around the world or something?" said Bugsy.

"I *was* flying around the world," she replied. "I don't know exactly what happened. I was in the middle of the Pacific. I seem to remember blacking out, and then—well, here I am in someone's parlor."

"That's funny," said Bugsy. "The last thing *I* remember is a coupla Al Capone's goons comin' after me with machine guns, and then nothing. And here *I* am in somebody's livin' room, too." He looked Amelia/Marigold up and down. "But I'm sure glad to be here with a doll like you, baby."

"I beg your pardon!" said Amelia, flaring up. "Baby, indeed. I'm a married woman! I think an apology is in order!"

Marie leaned over to Eddie. "Even in past lives they couldn't get along," she whispered.

Eddie shook his head. "This is insane. I never believed in past lives in the first place."

Ozzie's voice came out of the phone again. "Hello? Hello?"

"Yes!" said Marie. "What do we do now?"

"Keep an eye on them while I think. At least

130

this past-lives phenomenon has bought us some extra time. They can keep on going back to past lives for quite a while. It should be quite safe. It should also be quite interesting for you."

Interesting? thought Marie.

The vibrating began again.

"Uh-oh," said Eddie. "Here it comes again."

They stood there and waited as the house vibrated, and their teeth rattled, and their innards were shaken around. Norton and Marigold stood there too, looking more or less normal except that odd expressions and twitches passed rapidly over both their faces like clouds in a windy sky, and occasionally their eyes rolled up so only the whites were showing.

The vibrating stopped at last.

"I guess they're poofing together now," whispered Marie, watching carefully to see who her parents had become.

"Lor'," said Norton in a Cockney accent. "Ain't this just ducky, though? Oi'm sure oi don't know where oi am!" He scratched his head.

"*Ach!*" exclaimed Marigold, staring around her. "*Wo bin ich, denn? Was ist dieser Platz?*"

"'Allo, what's this? A Jerry!" said Norton. "Oi'm in some strange place with a bleedin' German girl, oi am!"

Marigold crossed her arms and glared at Norton.

"Hello," said Eddie to Norton. "Can I ask what your name is?"

"Sebastian Enright, tinsmith, at your service," was the reply. "Where am oi, boy?"

"You're in Brooklyn, New York," said Eddie.

"Blimey," said Norton/Sebastian. "Oi ain't never left London in me 'ole life!"

Marie remembered that Ozzie was still on the phone. "Dr. Regenbogen," she said.

"You can call me Ozzie."

"Okay. Ozzie. How do you say hello in German?"

"*Guten Tag,*" said Ozzie.

Marie turned to Marigold. "*Guten Tag,*" she said.

"*Guten Tag,*" Marigold replied, looking suspicious. "*Wo bin ich?*"

"She wants to know where she is," translated Ozzie.

"New York," said Marie, wondering if they called it that in German.

"New York!" gasped Marigold. "*Ach, du lieber!*" She put her hand to her heart.

The house began vibrating once again.

"It's happening faster," remarked Ozzie. "That

**132**

means the pace will keep accelerating. I think they'll be poofing very quickly soon."

As soon as the vibration stopped, Marigold grabbed a yardstick from the desk and leaped onto the arm of the flowered sofa. She began screaming fiercely in a language that was completely unintelligible to Marie and Eddie. Norton, meanwhile, cowered in terror in the corner of the room.

"She's speaking Japanese," said Ozzie calmly. "Hold the phone up. Let me hear what she's saying." He listened for a moment. "She would appear to be a samurai warlord," he pronounced. "Definitely a man. Probably 1700s."

"Hai!" yelled Marigold, brandishing the yardstick menacingly.

"Eee!" screamed Norton. Then he too began talking very fast in a language Marie and Eddie had never heard before.

"That's Zulu," said Ozzie into the phone. "An African language. I'm afraid my Zulu is not very good."

The house began vibrating again. "Stop!" Marie yelled to the walls. "I can't take this any more! Stop!"

The vibrating, as if in response to her plea, stopped abruptly.

Marigold was still crouched on the arm of the sofa, but she looked very different now. She was holding her arms bent and close to her body, and her hands were curved in a clawlike way. Her neck was craned out, and when she saw Eddie, she cocked her head curiously.

"Awwwk," she said, tilting her head the other way.

"Good Lord, she's a—" faltered Eddie.

"—A bird!" cried Marie. "She was a bird in a past life!"

"Maybe she wasn't a very good person in the life before that one," remarked Ozzie. "Maybe she had to do a stretch as a bird, as a sort of punishment. Who knows?"

"Brawwwk," said Marigold.

"Forsooth," said Norton. "What is this place, my good lady?" He bowed deeply to Marie.

"New York," said Marie.

"New York," he said, rubbing his chin. "I am well acquainted with York. I am a Yorkshireman myself. The uncle of my grandfather was an advisor to Richard, Third Duke of York, before that good gentleman's untimely demise. But *New* York—that is a place I do not know. Odsbodkins," he added, staring at the telephone Marie was holding, "—methinks I am in a very foreign land indeed, far from England in the year of our Lord 1627, which I so lately left."

"Golly," said Marie, looking at her father in wonderment.

"Awwwk," said Marigold.

The vibrating began again, and it was harder this time.

"Ozzie, can't we do something?" Marie said. "I don't know how long they can keep doing this. What if they turn into cave people? What if they keep going, *before* that? What are they going to be, anyhow?"

When the vibrating stopped, Norton was speaking Chinese and Marigold was speaking Spanish. Ozzie listened briefly to what she was saying.

"Spanish Inquisition," he explained to Marie. "It seems she was an inquisitor. Late 1400s, most likely. She was a man again. Tortured people until they confessed to things they didn't do. That's why she had to come back as a bird."

Norton chattered away in Chinese. "Your father's a woman," said Ozzie. "Empress's lady-in-waiting, it sounds like."

Then the house was vibrating again. The intervals between poofs were getting shorter and shorter.

135

The next succession of past lives flickered by so quickly that there wasn't even time to figure out what they were. Marie heard French, Persian, something that might have been Mongolian, and finally, grunting.

Then Norton and Marigold were crouched on the living room floor, poking each other irritably and sort of growling.

"Ozzie, I'm scared!" said Marie. "What's going to happen?"

"I've just had a thought," said Ozzie.

"You did?" she cried. "Eddie, Ozzie just had a thought!"

"He had a thought? Great!" Eddie was watching Norton and Marigold to make sure they didn't hurt each other. Marigold appeared to be inspecting Norton's scalp for fleas.

"Yes, I've had a thought," said Ozzie. "It may not mean anything, but then again, it may."

"Anything!" said Marie. "Whatever it is, we'll try it."

"Well," said Ozzie slowly, "it seems to me that your father once mentioned in passing that your mother is always setting the clocks two minutes ahead in your house."

"Yes, that's right," said Marie. "She always does that. My dad is always late everywhere, so

136

my mother figures that if the clocks are a little ahead, that might just make him move faster sometimes, if he forgets she set them fast. She hates it when they get places late. In fact, she even told me a secret once—that she'd monkeyed around with the mechanism of the clock in the kitchen so that it would run too fast. When it got too far ahead, she'd put it right again, but he'd never really know exactly what time it was. She thought it would keep him on his toes."

"Mmm-hmm," said Ozzie.

"Mmm-hmm what?" said Marie urgently. "They're going to be at the dawn of time pretty soon!" The house had just been through another vibration, and her father was now bopping her mother lightly on the head with his fist.

"Was one of the clocks on the time machine the kitchen clock?" asked Ozzie.

"I don't know." She turned to Eddie. "Run downstairs and see if one of the clocks on the time machine is the kitchen clock, okay?" she said.

"Right," said Eddie, and sprinted for the cellar door.

Marie waited for a long minute, watching her parents pick at the living room carpet.

"Yes," called Eddie. "The one on Mom's side of the machine."

"Aha," said Ozzie with satisfaction.

"Aha?" said Marie. Nothing seemed very aha to her.

"Aha indeed," said Ozzie. "There's your problem. You see, your father set the clocks to be perfectly synchronized, exactly the same. BUT—your mother's kitchen clock was sneakily getting faster and faster. By the time your parents took their time trip, it was probably off by about seventy-three seconds. The two clocks were out of synch. And there it is."

"There is what?" asked Marie.

"It would have created time interference waves. Very nasty things, they are. You see, your parents planned to be rowing along nicely on the waves of time. But instead, they ended up on something like a rug that is being shaken violently by a large person who's holding it at one end. And that motion is actually pushing them backward. That's why they're regressing like this."

Ozzie sounded very pleased with himself.

"But what does this mean? Can we save them before they poof back too far?"

"Interesting question," said Ozzie. "Very interesting."

"Ozzie, you have to help us! These are our parents! We'll be orphans if you don't help us!"

Marie started to cry. She was embarrassed to be crying in front of Ozzie, but she couldn't help it.

Ozzie's voice actually softened and sounded almost human. "There, there," he said. "There, there."

Somehow hearing Ozzie attempt to have feelings was almost heartrending.

"Let me think about it for a few minutes," he said. "I may be able to come up with a solution. I'll call you back."

"Please, please call back very soon," Marie begged. "They're licking the rug. And they're poofing every minute or so now!"

# 15 OZZIE GETS IT

After she hung up, Marie tried to explain to Eddie what had happened. This was difficult, because Norton and Marigold had become interested in Marie and were checking her hair for lice.

"Oooh. Oooh," said Marigold.

"Eee-ee-eee," replied Norton. Then he poked Marigold with his elbow.

The phone rang.

"Okay," said Ozzie, without any preliminaries. "I think I may have something."

"Oh, thank God!" said Marie. "Eddie, Ozzie thinks he might have something!"

"Now, listen carefully. There are a few things you'll have to do, all right? Can you pay close attention to what I say? This may be very difficult."

"We'll do it," said Marie. "Just tell me."

"Do you remember what the time hum sounded like, the one your parents were humming when they rowed off into their pasts?"

Marie bit her lip. "I don't know. Maybe . . ."

She tried humming a couple of hums. "Hmmmmmmmmmmmmm," she went. No, that wasn't right. "Eddie, do you remember how the time hum went?"

"Sure," said Eddie. "It went, 'Hmmmmmmmmmmmmm.'"

"That's it!" shouted Marie. "That's it! Eddie, you're a genius!"

"No, I'm just interested in these things," said Eddie modestly.

"That sounded right," said Ozzie. "Now, here's what you'll have to do. First, change that clock on the time machine, the kitchen clock that runs too fast. Get another one, one that you're sure runs right. Buy one if you have to."

"Okay."

"Then, wire it to the machine in place of the other. It's probably a fairly simple wiring job. Just look carefully at how the kitchen clock is wired up, and attach this one the exact same way. Can you do that?"

"I think so," said Marie. "Eddie can help me."

"Good. The next thing you'll have to do is get two other people into your basement to hum."

"Huh?"

"That's right. By my calculations, you'll need at least four voices, humming at top volume, to reach the decibel level required to pull your parents back to the present."

"What will they hum? The time hum?"

"The time hum, *backward*."

"Eddie! Do you think you could figure out how to do the time hum backward?" Marie asked.

"It'll take me a couple of minutes to work it out, but I think I can."

"Good," said Ozzie. "If the frequencies of the voice waves are the proper ones, we'll be all right. If they're not, well . . . we'll cross that bridge when we come to it."

"Okay," said Marie. "I think we can do what you said so far. Is there anything else?"

"Yes," said Ozzie. "The last part is the most difficult of all. I don't know whether you'll be able to do it."

"Whatever it is, we'll do it. We have to. What is it?"

"You have to get your parents strapped into those rowing machines and rowing while your time hum chorus is humming."

Marie watched Norton inspecting the inside of Marigold's mouth. "Oh, brother," she said. "I don't even think they're cave people anymore. I don't know *what* they are. How can we get them to do that?"

"You'll have to find a way," said Ozzie. "Now, how long will all this take you?"

"I don't know. We'll have to call a couple of friends and see if they're free to come over. And we'll have to try getting Norton and Marigold down into the basement and rowing. I guess we'll just do it as fast as we can."

"Fifteen minutes?"

"That's awfully soon."

"Well, I don't want to alarm you, but if the poofing goes on for longer than eighteen minutes, I can't guarantee your parents' safety. By my calculations, eighteen more minutes will bring them back to the beginning—the earliest known form of human being. If they go back beyond that point, I just don't know what's going to happen. Nobody is really sure."

"Okay," said Marie tersely. "We'll get right on it."

"I'll call when you have all the elements assembled."

"Okay." They hung up.

"Eddie, you're not going to believe what we have to do," Marie said to her brother. Then she explained it all.

"I believe it," said Eddie. "It kind of makes sense."

"Why don't you run down to the drugstore on the corner and buy a good clock, and I'll call Lewis and Lila."

"Okay."

"And then we'll try to get them downstairs and onto those rowing machines somehow."

"All right. I'll be back in five minutes." He ran out, slamming the door behind him.

Hurriedly, Marie dialed Lila's number. "Hello?" said her friend.

"Hi," said Marie. "It's me."

"You who?"

"Me, Marie."

"You mean the Marie who used to be my friend? The one who used to call me practically every night, but now she doesn't call me at all anymore? That Marie?"

"Listen, Lila, I'm really sorry I've been so weird, but we've had some problems in my family. Big problems. I don't even have time to explain it now, but I really need your help. Can you forgive me and come over right now? It's life or death."

"Wow! Life or death!" Lila was excited. "Sure I'll come over. Be right there."

"Thank you, thank you, thank you! I promise I'll explain everything when this is all over."

"Okay, bye."

"Bye."

Next Marie dialed Lewis's number. His mother answered.

"Hi," said Marie. "This is Eddie's sister, Marie. Is Lewis there, please?"

"Well, he's here, but he's—um—indisposed, as they say. Can he call you back?"

Marie was jiggling up and down out of nervousness. "Gee, this is really sort of urgent," she said. "Could you get him out?"

Lewis's mother was taken aback. "Well, I, ah, guess I can. Hold on, all right?"

While she waited for Lewis, Marie stretched the phone cord a little tighter so she could see her parents. Norton and Marigold were roaming the living room, looking for something to eat. They kept picking up things like books and ashtrays and trying them out with their teeth. Then they'd make awful faces and grunting sounds. It suddenly occurred to Marie that her parents hadn't eaten in quite a while. But then again, what was quite a while? What kind of time were they operating on? Had it been a few hours, or a million years?

At last, Lewis came to the phone. "Hello?" he said.

"Hi, Lewis. I'm really sorry to interrupt you, but Eddie and I need your help. Do you remember when you came over to help us out when our parents were sort of, sort of little?"

"Ye-ah." Lewis was beginning to sound cautious, even suspicious. The last time had been strange and dangerous and scary.

"Well, we have another little problem now. We need you again. Can you help us? It's really, really serious."

"Where's Eddie? I want to talk to Eddie."

"Eddie's not here right now. But he knows I'm calling you. Could you help us?"

"It's going to be something weird again, isn't it?"

"It's . . . a little weird," admitted Marie. "But it's not dangerous. To you. I think."

"Oh, great."

"Please, Lewis?"

Lewis sighed. "All right. I'll come. Can I eat my dessert first? I was just going to eat dessert. It's rice pudding."

"No! No, don't eat dessert! You have to come right now!"

"But I'm hungry."

"Lewis, you can eat dessert after you get home. Right now, you have to save two lives. Don't you

146

want to save a couple of lives? It's not everyone who gets that chance."

"Okay, okay, I'll come now. But I hope it doesn't take too long."

"I'll buy you a whole vat of rice pudding someday, Lewis. I promise."

"Okay."

"Bye."

There. That was done, thank heavens. That had been great luck: The only two people they could really trust, and both of them were home and free.

Eddie came in the door. "Got a clock," he said. "The man said it was very accurate."

"Good. Listen, Eddie, they're hungry. They're foraging for food in the living room. Should we feed them?"

Eddie thought. "You know," he said slowly, "this could be our answer. Maybe we can use their hunger."

"What do you mean?" said Marie.

"Look, we have to get them downstairs and rowing, right? That's going to be hard with a couple of Neanderthals. Food can help us do it."

"Brilliant," said Marie.

Eddie opened the closet. "What do you think they'd like?" he said.

147

"What did people eat back then? Raw meat. Leaves and stuff. I don't know."

Eddie took down a box of Twinkies. "Well, maybe they'll like these."

He took one of them out of the box. It was very stale.

They went into the living room, where Norton was gnawing on the arm of the easy chair.

Eddie broke off a small piece of rock-hard Twinkie and held it out to Norton. "Here, try this," he said.

Norton came shuffling over and snatched the Twinkie from Eddie's hand. He peered near-sightedly at it; he had taken off his glasses some time ago. Smelling the Twinkie all over, he scratched it with his eyetooth, and then wolfed it down. "Urrg," he said.

He made another grab for the rest of the Twinkie in Eddie's hand, but Eddie whisked it away. "Not so fast," said Eddie.

Marigold had now become interested in the Twinkie. She came shambling over, and Eddie handed her a little piece, which she scarfed down hungrily after a brief sniff. She, too, tried to grab more from Eddie. Now they were both standing in front of him, eyeing his Twinkie like a pair of wolves.

Eddie started backing up, keeping his eyes on them. He knew if he stopped watching them for an instant, they would snatch his Twinkie. "Grab the rest of them from the kitchen," he said to Marie.

He kept backing up, feeling his way along the walls behind him, until he had reached the cellar door. Then he gave each of his parents another piece.

"Oog," said Marigold. "Nnng," said Norton.

"Good, you like them," said Eddie. "We're going to get you right back to the present with these Twinkies." He turned and ran down the basement stairs, with Norton and Marigold following on his heels.

Marie, meanwhile, stuffed her pockets with the rest of the Twinkies. Then she ran down to the basement behind them. They were all downstairs. But something was missing, Marie realized.

"Eddie!" she cried. "The new clock!"

Eddie slapped his forehead. "Oh, shoot, I forgot it."

"You run upstairs and get it," said Marie. "I'll keep them busy in the meantime with Twinkies."

"Okay. I'll hurry. If they attack you, give them all the Twinkies."

149

"They won't attack me. I bet they have some kind of deeply embedded knowledge that I'm their child. They wouldn't be able to attack their own child."

"Don't bet on it," said Eddie.

Marigold lunged for the Twinkie in Marie's hand, letting out a shriek as she did so.

Eddie ran up the stairs three at a time.

In a minute he was back, and Marie was still in an uneasy standoff with Norton and Marigold.

"I think this won't be too hard to hook up," he said, looking at the clock on the time machine. "There's only three wires." He grabbed a screwdriver and pliers off the workbench and set to work.

"Okay, done," he said.

"Are you sure you did it right?"

"Can't be sure of anything," said Eddie. "We can't be sure this will work at all, or that it won't send them so far forward or back in time that we'll never find them again."

"I know," said Marie. "You don't have to tell me that, don't you think I know it? I just asked if you hooked up the clock right!"

"Sorry!" said Eddie. "You don't have to jump down my throat!"

"Well, I'm just a little tired and nervous and scared right now, okay?"

"Okay."

"I'm sorry I yelled at you."

"Okay."

Norton made a grab at the rest of the Twinkie while Marie was off her guard, and wolfed it down.

"I wish Lewis and Lila would get here," she said.

"How many Twinkies do you have left in your pocket?" Eddie asked her.

"Three."

"Let's try and get them on the rowing machines," said Eddie. "Time is running short."

"Got any ideas about how to do it?"

"Yeah," said Eddie. He climbed onto the left-hand machine and started rowing. "Give me a piece of Twinkie," he said.

"You're hungry *now?*"

"No, you doof. Just bring Mom and Dad over here and give me a little piece."

It was easy to get Norton and Marigold over to the machine. Wherever Marie and her magic Twinkies went, they went too.

Eddie rowed away, and Marie popped a little piece of Twinkie into his mouth. "Mmmm," he said with exaggerated delight, looking right at his parents. "See? Anybody who rows this machine gets a Twinkie."

Marie gave him another piece. Norton and Marigold watched all this with extreme interest.

Then Eddie stopped rowing, looked at Marigold, and patted the seat on the rowing machine beside him. "Here, you try it," he urged.

Marigold scrambled immediately onto the seat.

"She's one smart cave woman," said Marie, and gave Marigold a little piece of Twinkie.

Eddie picked up his oars and started rowing again, and looked significantly at Marigold. Marie popped a little piece of Twinkie into his mouth. "Mmmm," he said.

Marigold hesitantly picked up the handles of her rowing machine and pulled them experimentally toward her chest.

"That's good! That's very good!" Marie cried. "This is going to work!" She gave Marigold another piece of Twinkie, and Marigold started to row the machine. She made a funny noise deep in her throat. She went faster and faster.

"She's laughing! She likes it!" shouted Eddie.

Norton had been watching this very closely, and now he wanted some of the action too. He grabbed Eddie by the shoulder, threw him off the machine, picked up the handles, and began rowing like an Olympic champ.

"Urrf," he said to Marie, looking at the Twinkie in her hand.

"Yes! Of course you can have some!" she whooped. "Yes!" She gave him a big piece.

Norton and Marigold were now rowing wonderfully, side by side, while Eddie and Marie hugged each other and jumped up and down, laughing and yelling.

Then the doorbell rang.

"I sure hope that's Lewis or Lila," said Marie.

"Why don't you go up this time," Eddie said. "Leave me the Twinkies and I'll keep them rowing down here."

"I'm so embarrassed that our two best friends are going to see our parents in this state," said Marie as she headed up the stairs. "Stone Age people."

"We could blindfold them," Eddie called after her.

"That's crazy," she called down.

In two minutes, Marie was back. She was leading Lewis and Lila very slowly down the stairs. They both had dishtowels tied around their faces.

"This is ridiculous," said Lila. "I'm going to fall down."

"Just keep holding on to the railing, and feel the steps with your foot," said Marie. "Pretend you're blind. I'm sorry I had to do this, but I wouldn't if there wasn't a good reason."

"I can't believe I said yes again," moaned Lewis.

"Why is the house vibrating?" asked Lila.

"Don't ask," said Marie.

When the three of them got to the bottom of the stairs, they inched their way across the basement toward the rowing machines. *Whoosh, whoosh, whoosh,* went the machines.

"What's that noise?" said Lila.

"Rowing machines," said Marie tersely.

"Oooongh," said Norton to Eddie, begging for another piece of Twinkie.

"What's *that* noise?" said Lewis.

"Nothing," said Marie.

"Are we going to get hurt here?" asked Lila in a slightly shaky voice.

"I really, really hope not," said Marie.

"That's very reassuring," said Lila.

"You two just stand here and don't move, okay?" said Marie. "I have to get a phone call."

"*Get* a *phone* call?" Lila echoed.

Marie went over to the phone extension that was in the basement. By now she trusted Ozzie absolutely, almost mystically. She knew he'd call at the moment he had to call.

The phone rang. "Everything's ready," said Marie.

"Good," responded the nasal voice. "It's time to start the backward time hum."

"Okay, Eddie, it's time to start the humming chorus going. Ready?"

"Ready." Eddie stood before Lewis and Lila. "I'm going to teach you a little tune," he said to them, "and we're all going to hum it."

"You brought us over here so we could hum blindfolded?" said Lila. "That's the life-or-death thing?"

"Yes," said Eddie.

"I hate not being able to see," groused Lewis. "Eddie, this is stupid."

"It only *seems* stupid," said Eddie. "Okay, here's how it goes: 'mmmmmmmmmmmmH.' "

"That's not even a tune, that's just a—a *squiggle,*" said Lila.

"It's not meant to be pretty," said Eddie. "I'll do it once more, and then you do it with me." He hummed it once more, and then they tried it with him.

"That sounded right," said Ozzie to Marie over the phone. "Are your parents still rowing?"

"Rowing away," she reported.

"All right. Then, when I say go, I want you all to hum as hard as you can. You have to do it loudly. I'm worried that you won't get enough volume to counteract the Rigatoni effect."

"The Rigatoni effect?"

"That's what's happened to your parents.

Anyhow, if you can't hum loud enough, you won't be able to counteract the effect. You may need to add a booster wave."

"What's that?"

"Basically, just some extra noise. It would have to be a certain type of noise, something quite loud and harsh."

"Can we start?" said Eddie. "The house is vibrating almost all the time now."

"Yes," said Ozzie. "Marie, go over to the machine and set the chronometer to today's date, three minutes from now. Then press the big green button on the front."

Marie panicked briefly. "What's today's date?"

"August thirteenth."

"Okay," Marie ran to the machine and came back in a moment. "Did it."

"Start humming."

They started humming. The kids hummed, and Norton and Marigold rowed. Norton and Marigold seemed to like the tune; they grunted along.

"Louder," said Ozzie.

They hummed louder. The house vibrated harder. Every few seconds Marie handed Norton and Marigold pieces of Twinkie to keep them going.

It was very loud in the basement, but Eddie

157

and Marie became aware of a faint pounding from upstairs. They kept humming.

"It's not going to work," said Ozzie. "It's not loud enough."

There was a crash at the top of the basement stairs, and Mildred Grackle appeared. There seemed to be steam, or brimstone, rising all around her. She looked like a frizzy-haired demon.

"YOU!" she screamed. She charged down the stairs, yelling at the top of her lungs. "You have made my life a constant living hell! First I go on a wild-goose chase halfway across the country to find some evil friend of *yours,* because you've cast some kind of spell over me, and then I come home to find that my mushrooms are all dead, your house is vibrating, *my* house is vibrating, and you're making so much noise, *as usual,* that I can't hear myself think! Well, one of us is moving out of the neighborhood, and it's not going to be me! I have called my lawyer, and you are going to be arrested for being public enemies, and your parents will be taken off to prison and you are going to reform school, and you'll never be able to live in this house, or this state, again! This is total war!"

"Excellent," said Ozzie in that calm, nasal voice

of his. "The booster wave. Just what we need. Keep her yelling."

"How?" Marie said.

"Provoke her. She may just provide enough power to put you over the edge."

Marie looked at Mildred and tried not to tremble. Mildred could be really scary when she was mad. "Have a nice trip to Phoenix?" she asked.

"What. Did. You. Say?"

"I said, did you have a nice time with our friend, Ozzie Regenbogen? I heard he really liked you."

All the while, Eddie, Lila, and Lewis were still humming the backward time hum at the top of their lungs, and Norton and Marigold were still rowing.

Mildred turned several unusual colors: a whitish shade, then a sickly green, then a livid red. She had clearly gone past the point of words. So she stood in front of Marie, who was again humming, and she screamed. It was a prodigious, towering, immense, enormous scream. A speeding subway car whose wheels need oiling. A large opera singer stepping on a tack in the middle of a mad scene. The space shuttle taking off.

"That's it!" cried Ozzie. "The booster wave! Get ready, because here it comes!"

The vibrating grew louder and louder, deeper and deeper, very quickly, until it reached the same bone-rattling hum that it had when Norton and Marigold had first begun their strange journey. Then there was a very loud bang, which made poor blindfolded Lila and Lewis jump about a foot.

"It's done!" cried Ozzie. "Get them off the machine—fast! Quickly, quickly!"

Marigold had stopped rowing, and then Norton stopped too. "Marie!" she exclaimed. "What are you doing down here? What's happened? Did we travel in time? I can't remember."

"Mom! Thank God!" said Marie. "Get off the machine, quick! You too, Dad! Fast!"

"But I'm so tired," said Marigold.

"Ozzie says you have to get off *right now!*"

That did it. They began climbing off the rowing machines, and not a second too soon, because something strange was happening, something the likes of which Eddie and Marie had never seen before.

It was a sort of wave, a huge wave, a tidal wave of air that rolled through the basement. You couldn't as much see it as sense it, and it had tremendous power. It rolled the dust of the basement along with it.

"It's a loose time wave. Get out of its way!" directed Ozzie.

Marie relayed the message. "Everybody out of the way of the wave!"

Quickly, Eddie pulled Lewis and Lila's dishtowels down so they could see where they were going. Then he grabbed their arms and half-guided them, half-threw them into the corner of the basement. Norton and Marigold had enough presence of mind to follow suit, and all the Bickers dove for cover in the corner next to Lewis and Lila. Marie left the phone receiver dangling by its cord from the wall.

The invisible time wave was rolling slowly and relentlessly toward the far wall of the basement, kicking up dust as it went. Electricity crackled all around it. Its power was awesome. "Mildred, look out! Get out of the way!" screamed Marie.

But Mildred just stood there, screaming. She hadn't screamed herself out yet. She was busy.

The six people huddling in the corner of the basement watched the slow-motion scene before them in wonderment and horror. The wave reached the far wall, smacked into it with a thud, rebounded off the wall, and ricocheted back across the basement, picking up speed. It rolled right over Mildred.

She reeled backward with the shock of it, but remained standing. For a moment, it seemed that she was okay. But then her body started to shake all over, her eyes rolled up, and her face twitched. She let out one very large hiccup.

And then, as quickly as it had happened, it seemed to be all over. Mildred stood there, smiling benevolently at the six of them in the corner.

"Thank you for inviting me into your tele-shopper homes," she said. "Please don't touch that transporter dial, because I have an exciting offer to make you today. Are you tired of living thirty people to a room and breathing dirty earth air? Well, step up to the 2150s. Come to the moon—where there's only moderate crime, just a little pollution, and you'll weigh a lot less! Our craterfront lunar properties offer the best in modern living. You won't be sorry you made the move. These parcels are going fast, so grab one today."

The group in the corner looked at each other, stunned.

"What's going on?" said Lewis.

"We've poofed her back here from her next life," Eddie whispered.

"Huh?" said Lewis. "Is that supposed to explain it?"

"I guess she's going to be some kind of future real estate salesperson," said Marie to Eddie.

"A sleazy one," whispered Eddie. "Like the ones who sell swampland now."

"Poofed her?" said Norton. "What are you talking about? What does that mean, poofed her?"

"We'll explain it all later, Dad," said Marie.

Mildred had stopped talking. "This is a very unusual living room, if you don't mind my saying so," she said. "Where's your transporter? And where's your gas mask closet, anyway?"

"We're a little behind the times," said Eddie. "Can you excuse us a minute while we talk this over?"

"Sure," said Mildred. "Take all the time you want."

"What should we do with her?" said Marie.

"Beats me," said Eddie. "Why don't you ask Ozzie?"

"Ozzie!" exclaimed Marie. "I forgot all about him! He must still be on the phone!" She ran for the phone. "Ozzie?" she yelled into it. "Dr. Regenbogen?"

But he was gone.

"Oh, great," said Eddie. "Now what are we supposed to do?"

"We'll have to think of something until he calls again. Maybe we can figure it out ourselves."

"I have an idea," whispered Eddie. "Miss?" he said aloud to the Mildred of the future.

"Yes?" she said, turning back to them. "You can call me Ardis. Ardis Loophole is my name."

"Well, Ardis, we've been talking about it, and we don't think we're really interested in lunar property right this minute. But we know somebody who probably is. In fact, I'll bet she'll be very, very interested."

Mildred/Ardis's eyes lit up in a wolfish way. "Really?" she said. "Where can I find her? I'll teleport myself there right now."

"The good news is, you don't even need to teleport yourself over there. She lives right next door. She's not home now, but you can just walk right into her house. Everybody does. Just wait for her—she'll be back soon. Her house is over there." He pointed toward Mildred's house.

"I'll show you out," said Marie.

Later on, after Mildred/Ardis had been shown out, and Lewis and Lila had been thanked profusely, sworn to secrecy, and sent home, the

Bickers had supper. It had been a very, very long day.

Marie and Eddie took turns explaining the poof point, and everything else, to their parents.

"*Twinkies?*" said Norton. "I hate Twinkies!"

"I guess we'll have to figure out how to get Ardis back to where she came from," said Marigold.

"Ozzie will help us," said Norton. "We'll do it."

"I wonder where Mildred went when Ardis moved into her body," said Eddie thoughtfully.

"It's anybody's guess," said Norton.

"What I don't understand," said Marigold, "is what exactly started that Rigatoni effect, anyway."

"It started," said Norton, "because you loused the clock up, because you can never leave anything alone."

"Well, Mr. Eternally Late, I only fooled around with the clock a little because you're never on time anywhere."

"Maybe I'd be on time if I knew what time it really was around here!" Norton took a swig of his club soda.

"Well, they're really back," said Marie with a sigh. "Same as ever."

Norton hiccuped.

"Uh-oh," said Eddie.

Norton hiccuped again, and again.

Basil crawled under the kitchen table with his ears down.

"Oh, no! I can't deal with this!" said Marie.

"What's the problem? They're just hiccups," said Norton. "Give me a glass of water, will you?"

Marie rushed to the sink and brought him a glass of water, which he sipped slowly while Eddie and Marie watched, holding their breath.

He finished the glass. "They're gone," he said. "See?"

Eddie and Marie let out their breath.

"Welcome home, Mom and Dad," said Marie.

ELLEN WEISS and MEL FRIEDMAN are a husband-and-wife team. They've written *The Tiny Parents* (the prequel to *The Poof Point*) and *The Adventures of Ratman*, both IRA-CBC Children's Choices. Ellen Weiss and Mel Friedman live in New York City with their daughter, Nora, and their dog, Gracie. They've never invented anything.

*Uh-oh! There's been a BIG mistake!*

# THE TINY PARENTS

by Ellen Weiss and Mel Friedman

Eddie and Marie Bicker's parents have always been a little...unusual. They'll never win any prizes for housekeeping. They squabble constantly. And they spend all their time in their basement laboratory, working on oddball inventions. But when one of their experiments goes haywire, Mr. and Mrs. Bicker give new meaning to the word *weird*. They start shrinking—and before you can say "Tom Thumb," they're smaller than your average salt shaker. Worse, they've got the speeded-up metabolisms (and shortened life spans!) of very small creatures. Poor Eddie and Marie. They've got to find a way to get their tiny parents back to life size—and soon!

An IRA-CBC Children's Choice

A BULLSEYE BOOK PUBLISHED BY RANDOM HOUSE, INC.

*The fool of the school...*

# DOGS DON'T TELL JOKES

by Louis Sachar

Gary Boone knows that he was born to be a stand-up comedian. He spends his days joking around in school and his nights dreaming about fame and fortune. Unfortunately, all the other kids in his class think he's a dork.

Then the Floyd Hicks Junior High School Talent Show is announced. Gary's sure it's going to be his big break. Not only will he be able to show his classmates that he's not just your average class clown—there's that $100 prize, too. But while Gary's perfecting his routine, his classmates are figuring out ways to ruin him. Can he turn it around so the joke's on them—or is his debut destined for disaster?

"Readers will laugh at Gary's good jokes and groan at his clunkers."

—*Booklist*

"Will please Sachar's longtime fans and gain him new followers as well."

—*Publishers Weekly*

**A BULLSEYE BOOK PUBLISHED BY RANDOM HOUSE, INC.**